"I do lo[...]"

O'Mara was talking softly, touching her softly. His fingers rubbed the satin of Jo's teddy against her body so that she was caressed twice over. His hands went to her hair and began to unwind the silken cord that bound it.

Dark waves of her hair were released, and waves of passion were rolling through her, one lapping over the next.

"Ah, Jo . . ." O'Mara murmured, dropping to his knees in front of her.

"Yes," she responded hungrily, cradling his head against her, bending to kiss his hair.

Finally he drew back and slowly pulled her with him to the plush carpeting. "Whatever I've done to deserve you, love, I hope I can keep doing it. . . ."

Mary Jo Territo wanted to wow her Temptation readers with the romantic romp of two very unlikely lovers—and she has! *No Passing Fancy* is an accurate reflection of the author herself, her sense of humor and love of challenge. Mary Jo had a go at professional acting and book editing before she found her niche as a full-time author. She has also written under the pseudonyms Kathryn Belmont, Kate Belmont and Gwen Fairfax.

Books by Mary Jo Territo

HARLEQUIN TEMPTATION
52–JUST FRIENDS
111–CATCH A RISING STAR
121–THE VITAL INGREDIENT

HARLEQUIN SUPERROMANCE
190–TWO TO TANGO

Don't miss any of our special offers. Write to us at the following address for information on our newest releases.

Harlequin Reader Service
901 Fuhrmann Blvd., P.O. Box 1397, Buffalo, NY 14240
Canadian address: P.O. Box 603,
Fort Erie, Ont. L2A 5X3

No Passing Fancy

MARY JO TERRITO

Harlequin Books

TORONTO • NEW YORK • LONDON
AMSTERDAM • PARIS • SYDNEY • HAMBURG
STOCKHOLM • ATHENS • TOKYO • MILAN

Published February 1987

ISBN 0-373-25242-0

1

Jo Sherbourne raced down the hall and skidded to a stop in front of Studio C. Through the small, rectangular window on the door, she peered anxiously at the clock on the wall of the studio. Nine fifty-nine and twenty-eight seconds. Whew! She'd made it, with thirty-two seconds to spare. At the Metropolitan Ballet no one, but no one, was late for a class or a rehearsal. Especially the teacher.

Jo's already uneasy mood took a nosedive as she looked at her students for the first time. The scene in the room was startlingly different from the one that she, as one of the company's principal ballerinas, knew so well. No lithe dancers swathed in ancient woolen sweaters and leg warmers stretching morning-stiff muscles or stuffing down sugary doughnuts. No chatter and gossip about the previous night's performance. Instead there was a big bunch of big guys looking unhappy, uncomfortable and uncooperative. Standing in small clumps or lumbering restlessly around the room, in holey sweatshirts and grubby gym shorts, they looked like nothing so much as a motley herd of rhinos.

Oy, Jo thought, putting a hand to her forehead. How had she ever let Mrs. Charles, the company's artistic director, talk her into taking on the job of teaching the entire starting lineup of the New York Empire? Twenty-two huge football players. One taller and more ornery looking than the rest.

One of the larger suddenly stirred from a recumbent position, rose ponderously and pawed laboriously at his broad and powerful chest.

I'm supposed to teach these gorillas how to dance? With difficulty Jo swallowed the lump that had formed at the base of her long, slender throat. Not one of them looked as if he weighed less than twice her well-toned one hundred and five pounds. The one who had just risen opened his mouth into a gaping yawn. To Jo he looked mean—and hungry. "Any one of these guys could eat me for breakfast—raw," she muttered under her breath.

If the large minute hand on the studio clock hadn't suddenly jerked into a perfectly vertical position, Jo might have turned tail and run screaming to Suzanne Charles's office, begging to be released from her new duty. But so conditioned was she by the discipline at the Metropolitan Ballet, where she had studied and danced for half her twenty-eight years, that she took a deep breath and opened the studio door.

As soon as she stepped into the room, twenty-two pairs of suspicious, sullen eyes were trained on her. Holding herself erect, she walked as slowly and as gracefully as she could to the center of the mirror that covered an entire wall of the spacious room. *Now I know why they name football teams after jungle animals*, she thought. *Lions and tigers. Oh my. . . oh, my.* She felt like a gazelle who had to make a pride of hungry lions forget they hadn't eaten for days.

Jo shivered a little but tried to dislodge the goose bumps occasioned by the scrutiny of forty-four very male eyes. She felt nearly naked in her pink tights and black V-necked leotard. Even her woolen leg warmers were useless against the onslaught of disarming looks, especially the ones that came from the black-haired brute who stood staunchly in front, clearly the leader of the pack. He was slimmer than most of the others, with blue eyes that would have brightened the night in any jungle, no matter how deep and dark. As she passed him, Jo felt her shivers disappear and her face grow flushed. A film of perspiration swathed her forehead. Though she kept her head averted, she knew he knew he'd gotten to her. From the corner of her eye she saw his challenging smirk, and she was furious with herself for letting the big bruiser affect her.

She stood her ground and squarely faced the group. Though none of the men said anything, they exchanged looks and gestures that spoke loud and clear. They shuffled and fidgeted, some nervously, some defiantly. Only the black-haired brute stood easily, visibly confident of his superiority over her, a mere ballet dancer. She stared them down until they all stood as still, if not as comfortably as their leader. Not bad, she thought, for a five-foot-four matchstick. She waited another moment before she spoke.

Her "good morning" sounded surprisingly and maddeningly squeaky to her ears. The merest crack of a smile creased Black Hair's lips, and she dropped her voice to its deepest tone. "Will you all come to the center of the floor and spread yourselves out facing the mirror. Make sure you have a clear view of yourself in the mirror."

There was some schoolboy pushing and shoving as the men jockeyed for positions in the back row. Black

Hair, as she had known he would, cemented himself front and center. "Not everyone can be in the back row," she said loudly, and began directing the men into lines, staggered to allow everyone a mirror view. Not that any of them—except Black Hair—seemed to want it. She wondered how many times in her career she had wished for a class in which everyone—herself included—wasn't hogging the mirror. And now that she had it, she'd give it up in a minute. A second. Except that she had promised Mrs. Charles, and no one ever reneged on a commitment to her. No one would dare.

When the men were lined up and quiet again, Jo hurried on to the teaching. Perhaps if she could get them interested in dancing they would drop their posturing, their reluctance and recalcitrance. She spoke slowly and clearly. "We'll begin by learning the basic vocabulary of ballet, the ABCs, so to speak, upon which all dance movement is built." When she saw that they had digested that much, she continued. "There are five positions—"

"I can think of more than that," someone said in a gruff stage whisper from the back row.

Jo turned beet red and fumbled for a suitable retort to stifle the sniggers and guffaws, but before she'd found one a booming bass voice filled the room.

"You're out of line, Jenkins. And you're fined two hundred bucks. Next wise guy gets fined five hundred. Any takers?" Silence cut through the room like the deadly quiet of the jungle after a war-drum call. "Now what do you say to the lady, Jenkins?" Black Hair prodded.

A mumbled apology came from a burly, red-faced redhead.

"Thank you, Mr. Jenkins," Jo replied, mustering her dignity. "And you, Mr.—" She turned inquiringly to Black Hair.

A wide grin came over the mobile, expressive face of the hefty man standing next to Black Hair. The grin turned to a titter, the titter to a chuckle, and soon everyone in the room—except Jo, who didn't get the joke—was convulsed with laughter. "You really don't know who this guy is?" the big man asked, incredulous, wiping the tears from his cheeks. "Why, this is only *the* most famous, most handsome, most rich, most best quarterback in all of American football. Mr. J. Fred O'Mara. Hired by our new and mysteriously unknown owner to keep the Empire from striking out again this season."

"That'll do, Rory," O'Mara said. He spoke good-naturedly, but Jo couldn't help but notice the red patches on his cheeks.

"I'm afraid I don't follow football, Mr.—"

"Washington," the man supplied. He eyed her skeptically. "You been living in a closet for the last few months? You didn't read anything in the papers about how somebody—could be anybody, could be the president of the United States, for all we know—bought up the Empire and hired J. Fred here to whip these poor hurtin' backsides into some kind of shape?"

Jo shrugged and smiled. "It's news to me, Mr. Washington."

Rory Washington shook his head, still unbelieving.

She was about to try to go on with the lesson when O'Mara turned to address the players.

"I know none of you wants to be here anymore than I do, but our contracts won't be worth the paper they're

written on if we don't get on with this ballet stuff. So
let's try to make this as painless as possible for everyone, including the lady here. Maybe when this Joe
Sherbourne gets here he'll—"

"But I'm Jo Sherbourne," Jo croaked. Inwardly she
groaned. On top of everything else, they were expecting a man to teach them.

"You?" O'Mara's big blue eyes bulged like the eyes on
a primitive sculpture. "They sent a woman to teach us?"

Jo felt her back arch in defiance. "Yes. I am Jo Sherbourne," she repeated. "And I'm a woman," she added
hotly.

A rich, sweet smile spread over O'Mara's face like
icing on a cake. "I am well aware of that," he drawled.

As ruffled as she felt by his look, Jo was determined
not to let that show. "And I am aware," she returned
calmly, "that you, Mr. O'Mara, and you, Mr. Washington, and you and you and you—" she pointed to men
in different parts of the room "—think you have nothing to learn from a ballerina. You think it's sissy stuff.
Nothing for 'real men.' Well, you can all outrun me and
outthrow me, but I'll bet a dollar to a jelly doughnut I
can beat you all in endurance, agility, the ability to
perform consistently and to recover quickly after an
injury. So if any of you think those things are important to your game, maybe you'd like to listen up here."
Wondering if she'd been a marine drill sergeant in her
last life—she'd never spoken to anyone like that before, much less twenty-two beefy football players—Jo
began to demonstrate the five basic ballet positions.

There were no further uprisings from the class, and
in a few eyes Jo proudly detected a glimmer of respect.
In J. Fred O'Mara's eyes she saw that she had risen from

the status of unworthy opponent to a worthy one, but an opponent nonetheless. That was enough for her— for now.

The positions that were as natural as standing or walking to Jo were awkward and clumsy to the players. The soft music played by the class pianist helped some of them to relax and begin to get the feel of the simple arrangements of arms and legs, but others found it nearly impossible to assume the positions and remain standing at the same time. They were used to using their bodies like tanks, and the delicate, precise movements produced a lot of furrowed brows, tense mouths and loudly muttered oaths. Jo circulated around the room, using her long, thin teaching stick to beat time or to reach out to relax a shoulder or change the angle of a foot or hand.

When she thought they had absorbed as much as they could, she sent them all to the *barre* and demonstrated a *plié*. She stood in first position—heels touching, feet turned out. Slowly she bent her knees, sending them out over her toes. When she could bend no farther without lifting her heels from the floor, she straightened up. "This is a *demiplié*," she explained. "It doesn't look like much, but it's deceptive. Not only does it stretch your Achilles tendon, which is important in preventing injury, but it's essential to jumping or turning."

She invited the group to try it themselves and counted out the rhythm for the exercise. The pianist began to play, and soon there was a roomful of men bobbing up and down like horses in a carousel run by a drunkard. Jo rapped sharply on the floor with her stick, and the pianist stopped. But the players contin-

ued to bend. "Whoa, there. Hold it." She rapped again,
and movement ceased. "The idea, gentlemen, is to do
it all together. Everybody down at the same time,
everybody up at the same time." Counting aloud to the
music, Jo demonstrated the exercise again. "Got it?"
She took the generalized grumble as a positive response.

The pianist began the Chopin *étude* once more, and
this time only three or four heads were out of synch
with the rest of the group. She counted loudly and
passed down the row, correcting and complimenting.
As she passed J. Fred O'Mara, he turned his head and
gave her a smug grin.

Jo bristled like a prodded porcupine. Just because he
had the best *demiplié* in the class didn't mean he could
look at her like that. "Eyes front, Mr. O'Mara," she ordered. "And don't grunt," she added sweetly. "Grunt-
ing is not graceful." The smug grin turned to a lethal
leer.

After teaching the rudimentary *barre* exercises, Jo
brought the men to the center of the floor again and
taught a simple sequence of steps. She drilled it over
and over and then divided the class into four groups of
five and one group of two, so that she could pay more
attention to each student as he performed the sequence. She made sure O'Mara was at the front of the
first group, always an unenviable place in any ballet
class. There was no teacher to follow, only your own
reflection in the unflattering mirror, and your fellow
students sizing up your every move. And Jo was certain no one wanted to be the first to perform in front of
his fellows today.

The first five took the floor warily after Jo explained what was to happen, a couple of them sending murderous looks toward their colleagues. Jo prayed that none of the watchers would laugh. She knew she couldn't handle a melee; in fact, she didn't know if the entire New York City Police Department could handle the kind of brawl these guys could probably produce. The first five, including O'Mara, were standing awkwardly in the middle of the big studio, looking small in the vast room despite their bulk. They shifted uneasily from one foot to the other, didn't know what to do with their hands.

"You have to be prepared for the start of the music, gentlemen," she reminded them. "Spine straight, head erect, right foot at the ready, resting easily behind the left, arms in first position." She showed them what she meant, and when all five were as ready as they were ever going to be, she signaled to the pianist to start the music. Two of the men floundered on the first step and never caught up. One made it through the first two steps before getting confused; another got halfway through. But only J. Fred O'Mara made it through the entire sequence. She could see him counting under his breath the whole time, but he completed the little dance and did it mostly in concert with the music.

"Excellent, Mr. O'Mara," Jo praised, genuinely surprised. "And not bad, the rest of you. But that was very good, Mr. O'Mara."

"A regular little twinkle toes, aren't ya, O'Mara?" one of the spectators ragged. There was a round of cackles and whoops.

O'Mara put him down with a withering look. "At least I can find my toes, Marconi, without getting confused," he shot back. The group answered with a louder round of whistles and catcalls.

"Please, gentlemen!" Jo yelled over the din.

"All right, knock it off, you goons," O'Mara ordered.

He started to leave the floor, but Jo called him back. "Would you mind, Mr. O'Mara, demonstrating the combination for us again?"

"You mean alone?"

"Yes. I think it would be very helpful for the class." If they could see that their leader could do it, it might give them all incentive to try harder and to take the class seriously. Besides, she couldn't resist putting O'Mara on the spot.

O'Mara started to say something but then gritted his teeth and gave a small, sardonic bow in her direction. He executed the combination again, getting the movements right and counting less tensely than the time before.

"Awwright!" Rory Washington called when O'Mara had come to a thudding halt at the end of the combination. The men clapped and whistled, but O'Mara's face darkened, and he drew his index finger across his throat in a sharp, deft motion. Not a further peep was heard.

By the time the other four groups had danced the combination, it was almost time for the class to end. Jo brought the entire group back to the center and taught them the simple bow that ended every class—from preschooler to professional level—at the Metropolitan Ballet. She had hardly finished saying, "That's all for today, gentlemen," when the stampede toward the door began. "Except for one thing!" she yelled at the runaway, raggle-taggle crew. "I expect all of you to be properly dressed for the next class—black tights, white T-shirts, black ballet slippers. No more holey sweat-shirts and grubby gym shorts like today."

"It's bad enough we've got to be here," someone griped, "but I'm not dressing up like a wimp. No way, José."

"Can it, Maxwell. You heard the lady." O'Mara turned to her. "Your wish is our command," he said with mock gallantry. There was a dare in every sylla-ble.

"These are merely the dress regulations of the school, Mr. O'Mara," she said with a coolness she hardly felt. "I'm surprised no one explained them to you before-hand."

"It seems there were a lot of things no one told me about, Ms Sherbourne."

As they were speaking the rest of the men filed quickly out of the room, and the pianist picked up his music from the piano and rushed to his next assign-ment, leaving the two of them alone. The room was strangely quiet; no sound could be heard, but echoes of piano music seemed to hover in the warm, moist air. Slowly O'Mara's eyes took in every inch of her, from the coil of dark brown braids on the top of her head to the small bony, feet encased in flat pink ballet slippers, missing none of the lines and curves in between. He stared for a long moment into her coal-black eyes and then, without another word, strode swiftly from the room.

Jo stood stock shock still for several seconds and then collapsed in a heap on the wood floor. She took several deep breaths, realizing that she'd hardly put any air in her lungs in the past hour and a half. But she'd done it. Gotten through the class. And not too badly. She gave herself a mental pat on the back. *Twinkle toes, indeed*, she thought with a giggle. She would bet Mr. J. Fred O'Mara wasn't too fond of that moniker. She could see him in the locker room . . . all those bodies. Her imagination ran wild for a second, and she broke into peals of merry laughter. She was laughing so loudly she didn't hear the door open.

"Jo, are you all right?"

Jo scrambled to her feet. "Fine, Mrs. Charles, just a bit giddy. Sorry." She secured a loose pin in her braid and tugged at the sleeves of her leotard. There was something about Suzanne Charles that made everyone try hard for perfection in every effort. Perhaps it was because she tried so hard herself—and nearly always achieved perfection.

"How did the class go?"

"It was a bit rough at first, but I think it's going to be all right."

"Why don't you tell me about it over lunch? You'll need a decent meal before the afternoon rehearsal."

The two women walked briskly down the hall—one always walked briskly with Mrs. Charles—and took the elevator to the company dining room on the top floor of the building, where Jo knew she would get the kind of nutritious lunch Suzanne Charles deemed indispensable to her dancers' health and stamina. But feeling just a little bit wicked—and as if she'd earned a treat—Jo wished she could have sneaked across the street for a burger and fries.

2

GO, GO, GO, Jo found herself thinking as she watched
J. Fred O'Mara barreling toward the end zone, free and
clear for the first time in the game. As he got closer and
closer to touchdown territory, she began to vocalize her
thoughts, quietly at first and then more and more
loudly, until she was standing and punctuating each
cheer with a punch in the air. She was so intent on
watching the Empire's first chance to get on the scoreboard that she didn't see the tackle racing to head off
O'Mara. Unfortunately, the rest of the Empire didn't
notice him, either.

O'Mara went down with a bump and a skid. He lay
without moving for a moment and then began to pound
the football into the ground in frustration. The rest of
the team didn't even know he'd been caught until the
crowd let out a tremendous, collective groan. The opposing team fell away, leaving the Empire players in
midfield scratching their helmets.

Jo turned in exasperation to Mrs. Charles, who was
sharing the unknown owner's box with her. "They just
can't seem to do anything right, can they?" All afternoon the Empire had lived up to their reputation as the
Keystone Kops of football. Only a few minutes of play
remained, and the score was a humiliating 43-0.

"I suppose that's why they need us, my dear," Mrs.
Charles replied evenly. "Or you, to be more accurate."

"What do you mean?"

"When you're onstage, don't you always know in your mind's eye exactly where every other dancer in the piece is?"

"Of course," Jo answered automatically. "Oh, I see. If the team had been aware of that tackle's position, they'd never have let him get anywhere near O'Mara."

"Very good, Jo. For someone who's never been to a football game before, you're catching on very quickly." She pressed the buzzer that was built into her plush theater-type seat, and in a matter of seconds the glass doors leading from the enclosed, climate-controlled box to the sumptuous suite beyond slid open. A tall, willowy man wearing sober black butler's garb slipped silently into the box.

"You rang, madam?" he inquired in a crisp British accent.

When Jo had arrived at the owner's box in Empire Stadium with Mrs. Charles, to be greeted at the door by Godfrey, she had nearly fallen over. Mrs. C, who had grown up in a moneyed family and was the widow of a wealthy Wall Street lawyer, had treated the man with the ease of one accustomed to servants. Not knowing what else to do, Jo had copied Mrs. C's behavior. Now, after having been excellently attended by the man all afternoon, she had begun to accept his unobtrusive presence as not at all unusual, but just what one would expect when being entertained by the Emperor—as she had dubbed the mysterious owner of the New York Empire while enjoying his unstinting hospitality.

"My coat, please, Godfrey," Mrs. Charles requested.

"Certainly, madam."

"You can't leave now," Jo cried. "The game isn't over. How will I know what's going on?"

"Just keep your eye on the ball—and the quarterback, my dear. He's a handsome young man, isn't he? I'm afraid duty calls. Buffy Sproul is giving a cocktail party, and some of our most important patrons will be there, so I mustn't miss it. You stay as long as you like. I'm sure Godfrey will take good care of you."

Godfrey appeared with Mrs. Charles's midnight-black mink, and she rose gracefully to don it. Though she'd been sitting all afternoon, there wasn't a wrinkle in her perfectly tailored Italian silk dress or a single blond hair escaping the sleek bun at the nape of her smooth, taut neck. As she slipped her arms into the satin-lined sleeves of her elegant coat, the diamonds on her fingers and wrists caught the afternoon sun.

The flash cut across Jo's eyes, evoking a pang of envy. It wasn't Mrs. C's mink or the diamonds Jo coveted; it was her ease, her graciousness, the way she was never ruffled or rushed, no matter what crisis arose or what disaster loomed. In a dance class or a performance, Jo had grace and confidence in abundance, but in so many other situations she just couldn't get her act together.

As she stood by the glass door watching Mrs. Charles cross the sumptuous suite, Jo's feet, as if acting independently of their owner, assumed first position and did a series of *petits battements* and a few *ronds de jambe*. She was about to finish off her impromptu exercises with a couple of *demipliés* when she noticed the eerie quiet that had taken over the stadium. The clamor had died down; the fans seemed to be holding their collective breath.

Jo rushed to the front of the box, slid open the Plexiglas door and stepped onto the small balcony. The Empire line was assembled just inches from the goal. The linesman's stanchion showed it was fourth down; there were only seconds left on the clock. Jo saw O'Mara move his arm, and the next thing she knew there was an enormous pileup on the field. The players were stacked one on top of another like wood for a bonfire. It was impossible to tell what was going on. She looked for the zebra-shirted referee, hoping to see him to raise arms over his head, but by the time she'd spotted him the whistle signaling the end of the play had sounded. The season was four weeks old, and the Empire had yet to get on the scoreboard—despite the best efforts of one J. Fred O'Mara.

The crowd let loose with a barrage of disgruntled hisses and boos. Heads hanging, shoulders sagging, the Empire filed off the field, except for O'Mara, who was stomping up and down in the end zone, punching one hand so violently into the other that Jo imagined she could hear the thud all the way to the fifty-yard line, above which the owner's box was perched. With a final, mulelike back kick to the goalpost, the quarterback left the field, too.

Jo propped her right leg up on the balcony railing and stretched over it, resting her chin on her knee, watching the crowd file dejectedly from the stands. She'd been surprised to see that the stadium was full this afternoon, as she'd always heard that losing teams don't attract many followers. But Mrs. C had told her that the acquisition of J. Fred O'Mara and his long-time receiver Rory Washington had caused a big boost in attendance.

Jo changed position, rotating her torso sideways so that her right ear was resting on her knee and her left arm was stretched over her head. She'd also been surprised to find that Mrs. C knew so much about football. But it seemed that the late Mr. Charles, Oliver, had played for Harvard and had been a fan of the Empire; he had also been a friend of the team's previous owner. Mrs. C had even been in the owner's box before—when it hadn't been so "delightfully furnished and staffed," as she'd put it.

She really seemed to have enjoyed herself today, Jo thought as she hoisted her left leg onto the railing and bent sideways over it. But then Mrs. C always did. Even that night when the cast had had to be changed at the last minute because of an injury and the lighting board had gone on the fritz and the costume mistress had eloped twenty minutes before curtain time, Mrs. C had not only kept her temper and her cool, but her zest, as well. Jo admired her more than anyone she'd ever known.

The stadium was nearly empty now, and Jo was thinking idly that she ought to be leaving, getting back to her apartment. There were tights and leotards to wash for the coming week and music to learn. It wasn't often that she gave up a Sunday afternoon, usually the only free time she had. She stood upright and flicked her thick dark hair, which she'd worn loose today, over her shoulder. It hung down her back in gentle waves, covering the mauve angora sweater that clung to her slim frame. She adjusted the wool challis skirt that had gone askew while she was stretching and wiggled her toes in her buttery-soft leather boots.

Just as she turned and was about to leave the balcony, she heard the door to the suite open with a crash.

"All right, where is he?" O'Mara demanded. He was still dressed in his dirt- and sweat-stained red jersey, bulging with shoulder pads. His hair stuck out from his head in angry spikes, and the hollows beneath his eyes were menacingly blackened with burnt cork. He resembled nothing so much as a charging bull.

O'Mara tore through the room, flung aside the sliding glass doors and tromped through the viewers' box to the balcony. He grabbed Jo's arm and practically lifted her off the ground. "What kind of a joke is this?" Suddenly his eyes widened, and he dropped her arm so quickly she nearly fell over. "Oh," he said in confusion, "it's you."

"Who are you looking for?" Jo asked, just as confused.

"What are you doing here?" he countered suspiciously.

"I just watched the game. I'm sorry you didn't—"

O'Mara cut her off with a growl. "Who else was here?"

"Just Mrs. Charles," Jo answered nervously.

"Who?"

"She's the artistic director of the ballet company."

"And who else?" His eyes bored into her like lie-detecting lasers, and she took a step backward.

"J-just me," she stammered.

He wheeled around and stalked through the viewers' box into the suite. "I'm not leaving," he proclaimed loudly, "until he shows up."

Jo followed him into the room, tripping over the small step up from the box. She stifled a strong oath. "Until who shows up?" she asked O'Mara's back.

"The owner," he snapped. "I had a message in the locker room that he wanted to talk to me up here, on the double." He flung himself down, sprawling across several sections of the extra-long sofa. "And I'm not leaving until he shows up," he repeated. O'Mara propped his arms under his head and crossed his legs as if to settle in for a long wait.

"Well," Jo said uncertainly, "I guess I'd better be going. I'll see you in class, Mr. O'Mara." She turned and took a step toward the door.

"Stay," he bellowed.

His voice stopped her like the sound of a gunshot. She whipped around, furious. "No one talks to me like a pet poodle, buster."

"So," he drawled through an amused grin, "you've got a temper, have you? Good. I've never had a hostage before, but I bet they're better if they have a temper."

"What?" Jo shook her head as if there were something wrong with her ears. She thought he'd just said hostage.

"This is a sit-in, Ms Sherbourne. Neither of us are leaving here until this bozo of an owner shows his face. I'm good and tired of this cat-and-mouse game—especially since I've been the mouse."

And so now you're the cat and I'm the mouse, Jo grumbled to herself. *Why didn't I just leave right after the game?* "You can't do this," she protested vigorously as she made a dash for the door.

She hadn't gotten halfway across the room when she was lifted up like a stick in the wind and unceremoniously deposited on the sofa. "Maybe I can't, but I am." O'Mara settled into his previous position.

Jo righted herself and sat stiffly on the edge of the couch. "This is outrageous," she muttered.

"Perhaps you might be more comfortable, sir, in some other attire." The butler's bristle-brush voice beckoned from the opposite side of the room.

"Godfrey!" Jo cried, and started to jump up. A vise grip at the nape of her neck sent her thudding back down.

"Who the hell are you?" O'Mara was astonished, and his grip relaxed, but not enough for Jo to escape it.

"Godfrey, sir, at your service," he answered coolly. "Unless I am to be part of your . . . protest."

"I wouldn't plan on going home to the wife and kiddies," O'Mara said roughly.

"I wasn't, as I have been engaged for the entire evening."

"Run that by me one more time, Godley."

"God*frey*, sir. I have been instructed, sir, to direct you to the shower and to the change of clothing that was delivered this afternoon. I've also laid a meal in the pantry—"

"On whose say-so?"

"I take my instructions from Mr. Chapin, sir."

"Who's that?" Jo piped up, surprised to hear her own voice. Throughout the exchange between the two men, she'd been aware of O'Mara's hand on the back of her neck, so hot it seemed that everything inside her throat, vocal chords included, had started to melt.

"Our fearless leader's lackey," O'Mara scoffed. "Claims he doesn't know who gives the orders."

"Is there anyone, sir," Godfrey asked dryly, "whom you'd like me to inform of this 'takeover'?"

Jo was seized by an uncontrollable fit of giggles. Without raising a finger—or even an eyebrow—Godfrey was quickly gaining control of the situation.

"Would you mind letting the rest of us in on your little joke?" O'Mara asked with exaggerated politeness.

"I was just wondering who was in charge here," Jo said blithely.

"Oh, you were, were you?"

Suddenly O'Mara was on his feet, and Jo was scooped into his arms and heaved over his shoulder. "Get on the horn to Chapin, Godley, and tell him that no one's leaving here until he delivers the owner."

Jo, having recovered from the shock of O'Mara's move, began to pound hard on his back. "Put me down, you ape!" she yelled. She tried to kick her legs, too, but as strong as they were, they were still no match for O'Mara's biceps.

"And see if you can get a line on Patti Pringle," O'Mara continued over her protests. "This might make good copy for her show. We'll see you later, old buddy. Ms Sherbourne and I are going to hit the showers."

"W-what?" Jo spluttered, nearly choking on the word. O'Mara moved past the butler, and Jo reached out and tried to grab the man's sleeve. "Help! Godfrey, you can't let him do this."

"My deepest apologies, miss, but I never engage in physical contact from which is it unlikely I will emerge unscathed. And if I may venture one more thing, Mr. O'Mara?" he inquired deferentially.

"What is it?" O'Mara shouted, and picked up his pace.

"You're headed towards the pantry, sir; the bath is in the opposite direction."

O'Mara whirled around so quickly that Jo's head spun. At least if she'd had a bit of warning she could have found something to "spot" on, a stationary object to watch to keep herself from getting dizzy. She raised her hands to her hot, aching head, wishing with all her heart that she'd left the stadium with Mrs. C instead of waiting until the end of the game.

She wasn't sure of much right now, but there was one thing she could be certain of. Suzanne Charles would never have let herself be carried off like a sack of potatoes on the padded shoulders of a great gorilla of a football player. Mrs. C would have had the cool to get out of the situation somehow. *Why can't I do anything right*, Jo railed at herself.

A new thought struck her as her view changed from one of deep-pile pearl-white carpet to that of red-and-gray tile. "Anna Pavlova preserve me," she muttered softly. The shoulders beneath her would soon be unpadded. And so would . . .

Jo began to beat on O'Mara's back as if it were a tom-tom. She screeched and wriggled and bucked. O'Mara just laughed and slammed the door behind them. In another second Jo heard the click of the key turning, followed by the sound of it being withdrawn from the lock.

3

"YOU CAN OPEN your eyes now," O'Mara called over the pitter-patter of water on tile.

Jo had news for Mr. J. Fred O'Mara. She'd had her eyes open for several moments, since she'd heard the opaque etched-glass door of the shower snap shut. The steam was obscuring even the outline of his body now, but a few seconds ago she'd caught sight of the molded contours of O'Mara's well-developed torso. And as much as she hated to admit it to herself, she'd had a hard time keeping her eyes shut and her head averted as she listened to shoulder pads and clothing falling to the floor.

While O'Mara sang in a lusty bass, Jo sat back on the slatted wood bench and took in her temporary surroundings. The bathroom was enormous, bigger than some of the studio apartments the kids in the *corps de ballet* called home. Besides the stall shower, there was a sunken tub with whirlpool, a sauna, a basin and surrounding vanity and a separate cubicle for the toilet. Like the rest of the suite, the bathroom was decorated in gray and red, the Empire colors, and despite all its amenities, managed to give off a clean Spartan feeling rather than one of opulence and ostentation. For its sauna and whirlpool alone any dancer—herself included—would have been tempted to treason or treachery. Whoever the "Emperor" was, Jo concluded, he had excellent taste.

"We might as well be friends," O'Mara ventured. "We may be together for a long time."

"Humph," Jo responded. "I'm in the habit of choosing my friends, Mr. O'Mara, not having them forced on me. In a locked bathroom."

"Come on, Ms Sherbourne, be honest. What else did you have to do besides spending the evening with a nice guy like me?"

"My laundry, for one."

O'Mara laughed heartily. "If it'll make you feel any better, you can rinse out that jersey that's on the floor."

"Even for you," Jo said haughtily, "that was a contemptible comment."

"Yeah, it was," O'Mara admitted. "I'm sorry. I take it back."

Jo was so shocked by his turnaround that she nearly accepted the apology; she stopped herself just short of responding. He said nothing more, and for the next few minutes all she heard was the sucking sound of soap being lathered and the burble of water sluicing over O'Mara's head.

"What do I have to do to get on your good side?" he asked.

"Toss me the key to the door," Jo answered without hesitation.

"I'm through throwing for the day. Come and get it."

She responded with prolonged, pointed silence.

"Forget I said that," he said after a while.

"All right," she relented. If they weren't speaking she'd never negotiate her way out of here.

"I was serious. I don't see why we shouldn't be friends. After all, we may be spending a lot of time together in very close quarters."

"You're really determined to stay here?"

"Until I get what I want. And I always get what I want."

"There's always a first time, Mr. O'Mara," Jo challenged.

The shower door opened a crack, and O'Mara plucked a gray bath sheet off the towel rack beside the door. A second later he emerged with it wrapped around his middle.

The sight of him gave Jo a jolt. He was magnificent—skin scrubbed and ruddy, blue eyes shining, black hair plastered to his well-formed head, a thin mat of hair on his broad chest. Each of his muscles was so well developed that Jo could have drawn it for an anatomy quiz. Being a dancer, she was no stranger to the wonders of the nearly naked male body, but among all the companies all over the world that she'd danced with, she'd never come face-to-face with a specimen quite like Mr. J. Fred O'Mara. She averted her eyes when she saw that he was enjoying her reaction.

"I'm serious about being friends," he said, caressing the last word. "Can't we at least drop this Mr. and Ms stuff?" He smiled invitingly. "All my friends call me O'Mara."

"And what does your mother call you?"

"What has that got to do with it?"

"Just answer the question, please."

"Fred," he said abashedly.

"I like that," Jo declared, stifling a broad smile. "I'll call you Fred."

"You don't really want to do that, do you?"

"Of course I do. Didn't anyone ever tell you that part of being friends is compromise, Fred?"

With effort O'Mara gritted his teeth against the name he had detested since infancy. "And what does your mother call you?" he inquired, hoping to catch Jo at her own game.

"Jo. Just like everyone else."

"All right," he said with a disarmingly charming smile, "Jo and Fred it is. I don't mind giving up a few yards if it means scoring eventually." He eyed her provocatively.

"I trust you're not using that term in the locker-room sense, Fred," Jo answered, trying not to lose her cool completely.

"Just a metaphor, Jo," he said easily.

Jo's face was burning, and she could feel beads of perspiration forming on her forehead and upper lip. It was getting far too hot for comfort in here. "This is a lovely conversation, but for those of us with our clothes *on*, it's getting a bit warm in here. I don't often take a steam bath in a wool sweater."

"I wouldn't mind getting out of here," O'Mara answered with a shrug, "but I'd rather not go in a towel. Think you can hand me those clothes?"

On a freestanding rack beside the wooden bench were hanging a pair of neatly pressed gray wool slacks and a blue silk shirt just a shade darker than O'Mara's eyes. On the rack's shelf stood a pair of black Italian cut loafers, a pair of black silk socks and a pair of briefs so brief that they looked to Jo as if they wouldn't fit her, much less strapping J. Fred O'Mara. *Not my problem*, Jo thought smugly, and handed O'Mara the clothes.

Then she bent her knees to her chest and spun around on the wooden bench.

He took his time dressing. The room was so quiet she could hear each slow movement he made as he pulled on the clothes. The pad of each foot as he stepped into the briefs and raked them over his legs. The glide of silk as he slipped his arms into the shirt and buttoned it. The snap of each sock as he pulled it over his ankle. The crush of wool as he pulled on the trousers. The sound of each tooth catching as he raised the zip; the soft whoosh as he slid one foot and then the other into the hand-sewn Loafers. She heard him walk to the vanity and splash on some after-shave; she waited impatiently for the comb he was passing through his wet hair to drop onto the tiled vanity top.

She listened for that sound the way she waited for the dentist to turn off the drill, knowing that the worst part of an excruciating five minutes would be over. Finally she heard the comb hit the tile, and she breathed an audible sigh of relief.

"Come on now," he taunted amiably. "I bet you take a lot longer than that to dress." He sauntered over and stood beside the bench. "Shall we go?" he asked, as if they'd been sitting in her living room and were on their way out for the evening. "I could sure use a drink and some chow. I wonder what old Godley has cooking."

"Godfrey."

"Right," O'Mara said, offering his arm. Jo stared him down, and he dropped it, unlocked the door and ushered her through it.

In their absence Godfrey had set up a small table next to the sliding glass doors, covered it with a red woven tablecloth and laid it with charcoal-gray stoneware, red-tinted goblets and burnished stainless-steel cutlery. On the low red lacquer coffee table in front of the sofa there was a tray of canapés, as well as a bottle of champagne chilling in a Plexiglas bucket. Godfrey himself stood at the ready beside the table, a white linen towel hanging over his arm.

"You can open that, Godfrey," O'Mara commanded. "And what about those phone calls?"

"Neither Mr. Chapin nor Ms Pringle could be located immediately, sir. Their respective offices are searching for them now." He applied himself to the champagne cork, and in a moment there was a muffled pop.

Jo sank onto one of the deep sections of the gray-and-black upholstered couch, and O'Mara plonked himself down next to her. Godfrey poured the champagne and withdrew to the pantry.

Before she could raise her glass to drink, O'Mara touched it with his. "You look damned attractive tonight, Jo," he said quietly. "I hardly knew you when I came in. It took me a minute to connect you with the drill sergeant in tights."

"Thanks a lot," Jo said tightly. She snatched her glass away and took a long pull.

O'Mara let out a labored sigh. "That came out all wrong. I meant it as compliment."

"Some compliment." Jo plucked up a puff pastry canapé and washed it down with some more champagne.

"Look, can we call a truce here?" O'Mara gestured around the room with his glass. "This isn't so bad, is it? Good wine, good food, nice room. Not a bad view, either. Ever see an empty stadium at night?"

Jo shook her head.

"Come here." O'Mara stood and waited for her to follow him. He was at least making an attempt to be human, so Jo went with him to the doors. He opened them, and they stepped out into the box. The Plexiglas door to the balcony was still open, and they went over to the railing.

The deserted stadium was an otherworldly sight. Just enough lights were burning for them to discern the outlines of the seats in the surrounding oval. Though there wasn't a soul to be seen, Jo felt as if the ghosts of thousands of fans were floating through the air. She listened closely and seemed to hear on the whistling wind a faint cheer, the echo of a voice over the loud-speakers.

"Weird, isn't it? Like being at a space station, waiting for the next rocket to land."

Jo shivered slightly at his words. She did feel as if she was a million miles out in space, even though she knew that the whole of New York City lay just beyond the stadium walls. O'Mara slipped an arm around her shoulders, and she stiffened a little. At the same time she welcomed the warmth of his touch.

"I like looking at the place when it's empty. It's just a piece of ground with some grass and some limestone lines now. No fans, no coaches, nobody expecting me to perform miracles. Puts it all in perspective."

Jo understood just what he was talking about. "I know. I feel the same way in an empty theater."

He turned her gently toward him. "So there is one thing we can agree on," he said softly. His hand went to a wisp of hair that the wind had blown across her cheek. He smoothed it back and ran his hand down the length of Jo's hair. "Maybe more than one."

Jo put her hand out to steady herself on the railing. She was feeling as off balance as if she'd lost a toe shoe in the middle of a performance.

"How about we see if old Godfrey—see, I got it right that time—has the chow ready? I'm ravenous." His eyes raked her body as if she were going to be dessert, and Jo came to her senses. The end to this meal would be whatever Godfrey served at the table. No matter what Mr. J. Fred O'Mara was cooking up in that pea-size brain of his, she vowed firmly.

They finished the champagne with their first course, a delicate spinach soufflé flavored with a hint of nutmeg. After clearing away the dishes, Godfrey opened a bottle of St. Emilion and left it on the table to breathe while he prepared the main course. Several minutes later he wheeled in a cart from the pantry and made a great display of finishing off, in a copper chafing dish, the Steak Diane, a tender filet of beef with a sauce of onions, mushrooms and brandy. He flamed away the brandy, carved the meat with a flourish and served them cleverly arranged plates: steak in the middle surrounded by a rainbow of sautéed julienne vegetables, green zucchini, orange carrots, white potatoes, red beets.

"This looks delicious," Jo said with genuine pleasure. Godfrey accepted the thanks he clearly thought he deserved and retreated once again to the pantry.

"You've got to admit I only take you to the best places," O'Mara said with a cocky grin.

"You had nothing to do with this," Jo reminded him. "And aren't you finding it just a little bit strange that on the night you suddenly decide to hold me 'hostage' in the owner's suite, there just happens to be a set of clothes that fits you perfectly and a gourmet meal waiting to be served by a butler who caters to your every whim?"

"Nothing surprises me anymore," O'Mara said flatly. "Ever since I signed this lunatic contract my life has been crazy. But let me tell you, I've got to find out who this guy is. It's driving me nuts. It's getting so I can't sleep at night."

"I have to admit it has me intrigued, too. As I was watching the game this afternoon I started thinking about him as the 'Emperor.'"

O'Mara barked with laughter. "That's pretty good." He looked down at his shirt. "And here I sit, wearing the Emperor's new clothes."

"Hardly that," Jo mumbled to herself, finding herself thinking about the emperor's new clothes, exactly like the ones in the fairy tale, that O'Mara had been wearing—or more accurately, not wearing—in the shower. She could feel herself coloring and tried to concentrate on her food instead.

Out of the corner of her eye, she watched him. Though obviously hungry he ate slowly, savoring the food and wine. Carefully dressed, sitting in the romantically dim light, he looked quite civilized, more than she—unfairly, she realized—would ever have given him credit for.

"I hear you're quite a dancer," he said suddenly.

Jo looked up in surprise. "Where did you hear that?"

"I had my manager look you up. He says you're one of the best—world class. Although some say you haven't received the recognition you deserve."

"I'm well respected," Jo said modestly. She was flattered, very flattered, that he'd gone to the trouble of finding out who she was. He had also received accurate information. She wasn't as well-known, especially outside the dance world, as she would like to be. Her partner, the Russian émigré Alexander Trevetsky, usually managed to occupy the lion's share of the limelight.

"Now don't take this the wrong way, but, uh, I was, well, I didn't figure from looking at you that you could be a great dancer," he said. Tact was not his strong suit, and it cost him something to get even these clumsy words out.

"Appearances can be deceptive," Jo replied, feeling kindly toward him for trying so hard.

"They sure can," he agreed readily. "I know you didn't think I would clean up so good and know how to use a knife and fork, but—" Jo tried to protest, but he cut her off. "It's all right. I'm not sensitive. A lot of women feel that way about football players. But we're just normal people."

"So are dancers," Jo countered. "Regular people just like everybody else."

"I don't know if I'd go quite that far. Some of you—" he met Jo's eyes across the table "—look better than 'regular' to me. A lot better."

This time Jo didn't look away but met his frank appraisal with a strong gaze of her own. The look lasted several long seconds before she started to feel flustered. *What are you doing,* she asked herself sternly. *J. Fred O'Mara is the last thing you need cluttering up your life.*

Your nice, well-organized, narrow life, her devil's advocate piped up.

Jo picked up her glass and drowned all her inner voices in a healthy swig of wine. *I'll pickle them all*, she thought vengefully.

O'Mara helped himself to more from the serving cart. "Not bad for jail food," he commented. "If you hadn't been here tonight, what would you have had for dinner?"

"I don't know," Jo said quickly.

"Come on," he coaxed. "Tell the truth."

"I honestly don't know," Jo said with annoyance. "I hadn't thought about it. Whatever was in the refrigerator, I suppose." She visualized the inside of her fridge, and all she could see was a piece of cold pizza, half a lemon and a bottle of flat club soda. "Or maybe I'd have ordered in some Chinese food. Why?"

"Curious. Wanted to see how this measures up."

"To what?"

"A normal Sunday night."

"I give it a ten for food and a ten for novelty. Okay?"

"And what about the company?"

"I don't like these kinds of games," she declared. She laid down her knife and fork on her plate and pushed her chair away from the table.

"Hey, I'm sorry," O'Mara said. "I was pushing it."

Jo walked over to the glass doors and looked out into the eerie stadium. She wanted to go home and wash her leotards and soak her aching feet. She'd had enough of J. Fred O'Mara and this whole stupid situation.

O'Mara came up beside her. "I apologize. I was out of line. I get that way sometimes. If I didn't I'd never be

able to do my job. I've got to push people around, look
for an opening. If I didn't—"

"This isn't a football field."

He held up his hands in a gesture of surrender. "Point
taken," he said. "Now come back to the table and have
some dessert. Please."

Jo ate a few bites of the glazed pear tart they were
served but didn't enjoy them very much. O'Mara tried
to be engaging; she was polite but didn't encourage him.
When they'd finished, Godfrey served coffee and
placed a bowl of chocolate truffles in the center of the
table. Jo tried to restrain herself. Showing enthusiasm
for the sweets could only play into O'Mara's hands, but
she couldn't help herself. Chocolate truffles were her
greatest weakness. She bit into one. It was the richest,
creamiest truffle she'd ever tasted. She let out an in-
voluntary sigh of the happiness only a satisfied chocolate lover can know.

O'Mara chuckled and gloated. "You've just given
away the suit of your trump card, Jo." He popped a
truffle into his mouth.

She reached for another. Somehow the bowl of truffles made his triumphant tone less grating, the need for
a snappy comeback less urgent. She took a nibble and
thought, but before she could say a word Godfrey announced that he had Mr. Chapin on the line.

O'Mara charged to the telephone and took it up. "I've
had it, Chapin. The owner shows his face here, or I
don't leave. I don't care how long—I'm in violation of
what?" His face got red, and he looked to Jo like a balloon in danger of exploding, but as he listened to Chapin he deflated. Slowly he replaced the telephone in the
cradle.

He came over to Jo and pulled her out of her chair. "Let's get out of here," he said gruffly.

"What's going on?" Jo asked.

"Never mind that. Let's go." He started to propel her toward the door.

"Hang on," Jo protested. "My purse and shawl."

O'Mara bellowed for Godfrey and waited impatiently while the unruffled butler brought Jo's things. Then he whisked her out into the deserted hall, down the private elevator and piled her into his midnight-blue Jaguar, closing the door with a ferocious bang. He zoomed off into the night, and not until they were cruising down the highway toward Manhattan did Jo think it wise to speak.

"What did Mr. Chapin say to you?" she asked tentatively, hands at the ready to cover her ears against a tirade. But O'Mara answered calmly, if tautly.

"They got me right where it hurts—in the contract. Would you believe they can fire me if I make any attempt to discover the identity of the owner? And if they do that I can't work for anyone else for five years."

"Why did you ever sign a contract like that?" Jo asked, flabbergasted.

"They're paying me the earth and the moon. And I never thought I'd care a twig about who this guy is." He chortled ironically. "When I made this deal I thought I had it made for the rest of my life. But it doesn't work that way. Something always comes up, doesn't it?"

"Yeah," Jo agreed. "It's a lot like trying to stuff too many things inside a suitcase. Just when you get one thing in, something else sticks out the other side."

They chuckled together and fell silent, more like old friends who didn't have to talk all the time than the ad-

versaries they had been. They had shared an experience—however absurd—and it had forged a bond
between them. O'Mara didn't speak until they'd crossed
into Manhattan. "Where do you live?"

"Seventieth between Central Park West and Columbus," Jo answered. "What about you?"

"I've got a place on the East Side where I crash, but
I really live on my farm in Dutchess County. I raise
horses—just a few now, but it's what I'm going to retire to after I get out of this rat race."

The revelation couldn't have surprised Jo more.
"I'd've thought you'd have become a sports commentator or a coach," she said.

"No way. And what about you? I hear dancers don't
last much longer than quarterbacks."

"Teach probably. Choreograph." She was only
twenty-eight. If her body held out, she had a good ten
years left. More if she was lucky. "All I know is dancing. It's all I've ever done since I was a little kid, all I've
ever wanted to do."

"You sound a lot more dedicated than me. I'm only
in this for the money."

"No one becomes a dancer for the money," Jo said
with a laugh.

They drew up in front of her building, a well-
preserved brownstone with a small garden in front and
window boxes full of yellow and white chrysanthe-
mums. The street was tree lined and quiet, and this late
on a Sunday night, almost deserted. Jo had opened the
door and started to get out of the car when O'Mara
reached across to stay her hand. "I'll walk you to the
door," he said firmly.

She waited for him to come around and help her out of the low seat, and she let him hold her elbow to guide her up the wide steep steps that fronted her building. She took her keys from her purse and let them into the imposing, wood-paneled hall. The door to her apartment was the first on the right. "This is it," she said, inclining her head. "I guess I'll see you later this week."

He moved so fast that Jo hadn't an inkling he was going to kiss her until his lips were pressed to hers. He held her so tightly she could feel her ribs straining against his arms, and the difference in their height was so great that her toes were only just staying on the floor. His lips were cool and sweet and had a taste reminiscent of dark, sweet chocolate and rich, heady wine. Images of the meal and the evening swept through Jo's mind like a forest fire, fanned by his kiss until they leaped and danced wildly in her mind. She threw her long arms around his back and returned the kiss avidly, fighting fire with fire.

Finally he released her and stood back. "I've been dying to do that for hours. But I'm glad I waited. It was worth it." He handed Jo her keys and without another word was gone. Even after his Jaguar had roared and torn off down the street, Jo was still standing in the hall, keys dangling from her limp fingertips.

4

JO FELT A LITTLE FLUTTERY as she walked down the hall on Tuesday morning to teach her second class to the Empire. She would still be very much on trial with the men, and she wasn't sure how her Sunday night encounter with O'Mara would affect her ability to control the class. If he'd bragged in the locker room to the others about Sunday night, she wouldn't stand a chance with them. Even if he'd been discreet, would he look at her in a way that would make the men sense something had happened between them?

Her own reactions were just as much a concern. Would she be able to forget his shattering kiss and treat him impartially? Would she recall the sight of him wrapped in a towel in that steamy bathroom every time she looked at him? As a dancer she was accustomed to the proximity of men clad in clothing designed to reveal their forms, but could she look at O'Mara in tights with the same objectivity as she looked at the rest of the men in the company?

She paused for a moment outside the door and took the same kind of deep, cleansing breath she took before a performance. *Think of them as a tough audience*, she told herself as she put her hand on the doorknob. *Win them over*.

She hardly recognized the men standing in neat, orderly rows, each and every one clad in immaculate black tights, black ballet slippers and white T-shirts. She hadn't expected such painstaking compliance with the Metropolitan's dress code. Nor had she expected last week's burly recalcitrants to have transformed themselves so completely.

O'Mara stood in the center of the front row. As she crossed the room to stand in front of the class, he watched her with twinkling eyes. There was the merest hint of something personal and private in his welcoming smile, but nothing she thought anyone else would notice. So far, so good, she thought. Her pulse's tempo had quickened at the sight of him, but she found herself enjoying the rush of adrenaline. Their encounter was a secret that fed her, as if it were a lovely underground stream only the two of them knew existed. She turned a bubbly smile on him and said good morning to her class.

"Good morning, Ms Sherbourne," they chorused as one angelic voice.

The team had obviously been coached, and it didn't take too much intuition to guess by whom. The all-too-innocent expression on their quarterback's face gave that away. *All right,* Jo thought, *let them have their bit of fun.* She grinned tolerantly and nodded subtly to O'Mara. She wanted to let him know she was perfectly willing to allow them their high jinks now if they took the rest of the class seriously. O'Mara held her eyes with a look that was a bit too warm for comfort, even in the cool, well-ventilated classroom. She wanted to look away, but he was too enticing, too compelling; she granted herself a split-second breach of discipline.

She didn't notice when he gave the signal, only knew that he must have given one. The entire team turned as one man, and she was suddenly confronted with a sea of T-shirts stamped with gray elephants in red tutus, red slippers with ribbons crossed at the ankles and red football helmets. Each elephant was curvaceous and coy, balanced precariously on one toe, attempting an *arabesque*. Each had a number on the bodice of its tutu and a name beneath the picture—a woman's name beginning with *E*.

The sea began to pitch and roll as the men moved this way and that. The team started to laugh uproariously, and it seemed an unpredictable hurricane had blown up; Edna crashed into Essie; Ellen collided with Ethel. O'Mara, hysterical with laughter, turned to lean on Rory Washington, and Jo saw that he had picked the most outrageous name for himself—Esmerelda.

Jo shook her head and waited patiently for the storm to subside. *Boys will be boys*, she thought. *With this lack of discipline, no wonder the team's at the bottom of the league.* Then it occurred to her that a lot of energy and effort and cooperation had gone into getting those T-shirts ready for this morning's class. "Very amusing, Mr. O'Mara," she said when the men had quieted down. "But the T-shirts aren't exactly regulation."

"You said we had to wear white T-shirts," he pointed out reasonably. "You didn't say we couldn't have something printed on the back."

"If you men could find a way around your opposition half as cleverly as you skirt regulations, you wouldn't be in the trouble you're in now," she said sweetly, her eyes and voice aimed squarely at O'Mara.

"The lady's right," Rory Washington said to O'Mara. The other men chimed in their agreement.

"So let's get to work," Jo ordered. The team shuffled uneasily. Having their bit of fun hadn't made them any more comfortable with the thought of ballet than they had been at the first class. If she didn't put them more at ease she'd never be able to teach them anything.

"Dancing is as much a discipline of the mind as the body, gentlemen," she began. The nervous stirrings diminished as she continued. "Dancers learn to command their bodies to perform difficult feats with seeming ease in order to create beauty, to interpret music and to communicate emotions and ideas. Those are the touchdowns we want to score, if you will." She saw as she looked around the room that she was beginning to make herself understood. "Strength and agility of body *and* of mind are the tools we use. You can add them to the running and tackling and blocking skills you already have. That's what I'm here to teach you. I'm not here to turn you all into Alexander Trevetsky."

"And what is wrong, Jo darling, with being turned into Alexander Trevetsky?"

Jo and the team had been so involved in what she was saying that they hadn't noticed Trevetsky enter the room. Even in the simple Metropolitan Ballet costume, the well-known dancer had a flamboyance that was impossible to camouflage. His white-blond hair fell engagingly across his broad forehead; his blue eyes flashed brilliantly beneath bold, arched brows; his cheekbones were high and prominent, his mouth sensuous, his self-assurance evident with every step, every movement.

Jo smiled indulgently at her partner. He had appeared at the class half an hour earlier than she had asked him to; he had upstaged her yet again, but it was impossible to be cross with him. He commanded acceptance and adoration with his mere presence. "One of you is all the world should be asked to handle, Sasha," she answered, calling him by the nickname that so often made magazine and newspaper headlines. He appreciated her answer as much as she had known he would.

"I am sorry to break in on you, my darling, but I could not restrain myself any longer." He took Jo's hand and planted a lingering kiss on it. "You know that since I am in America, sport has become my third passion. Only dancing and beautiful women like you come before it."

The team nudged one another, and eyes rolled. Unlike the rest of the men, O'Mara wasn't amused or embarrassed by Trevetsky's exotic manner. He had taken a sudden and strong dislike to the way the dancer treated Jo. He didn't like Trevetsky kissing her hand or the intimacy in his voice when he spoke to her. He had an urge to tell the guy to keep his paws off her. *What's wrong with me*, O'Mara wondered. *All I did was kiss the lady the other night. That sure doesn't give me the right to be jealous. Jealous? Whoa, fella, what's going on here?*

He was so caught up in his thoughts that it took him a while to realize Trevetsky was talking to him.

"I would be pleased to shake the hand of the finest quarterback in professional football today." Trevetsky extended his hand. "You are as much an artist in your world as I am in mine."

"Thanks," O'Mara managed, and offered his hand. If anyone else had said that, he thought it would have sounded incredibly conceited and self-serving, but coming from Trevetsky it sounded like a simple statement of fact. The dancer's stature also made the compliment that much more meaningful, he realized with some surprise.

Trevetsky then turned to Rory. "And you are Washington, the wide receiver. My compliments also to you."

Rory shook Trevetsky's hand. "I've never seen you dance, man, but if you do as well with the ladies as the magazines say, you must be doing all-l-l right." The team guffawed, and a few catcalls sounded.

"They exaggerate at times, but if the public likes it so—" Trevetsky shrugged, and he and Rory shared a laugh.

Jo knew she was fast losing the momentum she had started to gain before Sasha had burst in. She was just about to interrupt when he turned to her. "But, my darling Jo, I interrupt your work."

"We were just about to start the warm-up," she told him briskly. "Will you lead the *barre* work? Please line up behind Sasha, gentlemen, and keep an eye on him during the exercises. It will be easier for you to learn by watching his body than by watching mine."

O'Mara brushed past her. "That depends on what you want to learn," he whispered.

Jo reddened and opened her mouth to retort, then stopped herself. That wouldn't help her regain control of the class, and it would give O'Mara a pretty good indication of what she'd been thinking about him since she'd walked into the room. Better to play it cool. Her mouth curved into an enigmatic smile. "And from whom. I've always found Sasha a wonderful teacher." O'Mara looked at Trevetsky, and Jo could practically see the daggers shoot out of his eyes before he stomped off to catch up with Rory.

Why, he's jealous, Jo thought as she walked over to confer with the pianist. The thought pleased her. Plenty of people were jealous of Alexander Trevetsky for plenty of reasons, but although she had been among the jealous, she had never been one of the reasons. She had often envied his technique and his unfailing ability to captivate his audience, whether or not he was onstage. She had often felt eclipsed by him, especially recently, since she was now rising to the height of her powers as a dancer. O'Mara's jealousy—if she had read it right— was then doubly welcome.

While Jo conferred with the pianist, O'Mara conferred with Rory. "Just how hot is this Trevetsky?"

"Don't you read anything but those horse magazines? The man's on the pages of some gossip rag every week with a different dolly on his arm. Women from soup to nuts, my man."

They took their places at the *barre*. O'Mara was about to ask if Rory had ever seen a picture of Trevetsky with Jo, when Jo clapped her hands and called for attention. She reminded them about the *pliés* they had learned the previous week and counted out the series of exercises they would perform. O'Mara had to admit it was easier to do them while watching Trevetsky. He could see the way his knees were supposed to bend, how to keep his back straight, his behind tucked under. They didn't look like much, but these *plié* things were tough. He wasn't used to doing anything this subtle with his muscles, and Jo was right, it took mental as well as physical concentration to do it. Maybe that was where he was missing out in his leadership of the Empire: he wasn't asking for enough subtlety from the guys, wasn't asking them to do enough things they weren't used to, to extend themselves. That was worth thinking about and discussing with the coach. He also wondered if he were feeling more disposed to the ballet classes today because of Jo or because he was beginning to see that the Emperor's edict wasn't as arbitrary and punitive as he'd thought.

Jo circled the room, correcting and encouraging. The work seemed easier for the players who were used to moving on the field than for the ones who used their bodies like sandbags. She spent the most time with the tackles and blockers before calling the group to the center of the floor. She had thought about her teaching strategy the night before and had decided to get the men used to some of the most basic ballet movements before trying to teach a combination of steps, as she had last time. She would begin with a leap, the *grand jeté*. The dancer took two running steps, leaped on the third step, landed and repeated the process, starting on the opposite foot. It wasn't the easiest of steps, but it had a distinct-uncomplicated rhythm to it. Also, when mastered, it was fun to do.

She asked Sasha to demonstrate. One of the most extraordinary aspects of his dancing was the height of his leaps. He seemed to defy both gravity and time when he left the ground. Not only did he jump high, but he seemed to remain suspended in the air like someone in a stop-action photo. The men watched with a combination of awe and disbelief as he leaped across the room. When it was their turn, they lined up dutifully in the corner and tried to follow Jo's instructions, but most of them turned step, step, leap into clomp, clomp, thud.

As in the previous class, her prize pupils were O'Mara and Rory. They caught on to the step after only half a dozen tries, while the rest of the men were still having trouble. When she asked O'Mara to demonstrate, he didn't seem to mind being singled out as he had during the last class. He leaped across the room enthusiastically, if not as gracefully as she would have wished. But he made up for his lack of finesse by telling the team when he was through, "If I can do it, you can do it. All of you."

He cooperated with her next idea, too. Synchronization was an important part of dancing in groups, and she figured it must be an important aspect of successful football plays. She asked O'Mara and Rory to do the exercise together, trying to leave the floor at exactly the same time, jump to exactly the same height and land together after.

"There's more to this," she told the class, "than listening to the music. You've got to tune into what your partner is thinking and doing, anticipate his actions, match your own to them." O'Mara and Rory did the exercise three times, improving their performance each time. When Jo called "excellent" to them after their third try, they slipped each other high fives, and the team cheered.

Now we're getting there, Jo said to herself as the men jockeyed for partners in order to try the exercise themselves. *If O'Mara continues to give me support like this, I may be able to whip this group into shape, after all.* What had started as a duty for Mrs. Charles was taking on the fun and challenge of a new role.

Jo called a short break after the exercise was completed and sat down to rest with her back against the mirror. Sasha coaxed the team into rehashing the game that had been televised the previous evening. Soon the room was filled with vociferous discussion and demonstration. O'Mara wandered away from the group to join Jo at the front of the room.

"You seem to be enjoying yourself today," she said as he sat down beside her.

"I figured if I had to be here I might as well see if there's anything to get out of it."

"Is there?" She was aware of his closeness, aware of the warmth of his exercised body, aware of her own body clad only in its second skin of leotard and tights.

"There sure is," he said. He didn't elaborate. His mind was drifting back pleasantly to kissing her, and he was tempted to do it again, team or no team.

Jo had to turn away from his look. It was far too private a one for these public circumstances. As much as she was drawn to him, she didn't want to do anything that would undermine her ability to teach the class, especially now that she was beginning to see how helpful her teaching could be for the team and what a challenge it could be for her. She was glad to see Sasha approaching; any distraction was welcome.

"My love," he said, holding out his arms to her, "we must dance for them. Rory has asked for it; the team agrees. They want me to put my money where my mouth is."

Jo held back a laugh as she often did when Sasha used American slang. He spoke excellent English, but his accent was still quite thick, and colloquial phrases sounded comical coming from him. She put her hands

in his and hopped lithely to her feet. She hadn't planned
to dance with Sasha when she'd invited him to the class.
Mostly she had wanted the team to see that he was a
"real man" with a lively interest in sports and women.
Asking him to demonstrate exercises and perhaps perform a bit of one of his solos had been only secondary
elements in her plan. But if the men had requested a
dance, it meant they were becoming interested. She
couldn't refuse. "What shall we do? Something Russian and classical," she suggested. "Tchaikovsky. *Swan
Lake* or *Romeo and Juliet.*"

"Oh, no," Sasha protested. "We must do the *pas de
deux* from *Birdland.*" One of the company's most well-
loved ballets was set to the music of the American sax-
ophonist Charlie "Bird" Parker. Jo and Sasha had often
danced the principal roles together.

"All right," she agreed. The team might relate better
to the modern music and movements than to the dances
that were ballet's "meat and potatoes." Jo sent the pianist to get a tape of the music; meanwhile she and
Sasha limbered up and talked through a couple of the
difficult passages.

The dance started fast and lively, a spirited tussle between a man and woman. In the second segment the
music slowed; the movements became sinuous, pro-
vocative. Jo and Sasha threw themselves into the impromptu performance, dancing with verve and fervor
for their special audience.

The final section was especially erotic. Sasha lowered Jo to the floor, lowered himself on top of her; they
rolled and rocked for several bars before rising together, limbs still entwined, for the last difficult leap
and lift. Then they separated, danced to opposite sides

of the stage, ran toward each other. As Bird's solo reached its climax, Jo leaped into Sasha's arms. He raised her to shoulder level, holding her with one hand under her midriff, the other resting in the hollow between her back and buttocks. She tensed her muscles to make herself as light, as portable as possible, holding her own position—downstage leg bent at the knee, upstage leg extended, back arched, arms reaching above her head. Sasha whirled her around and ran "offstage" as the music died.

There was a burst of applause when they finished, even a few whistles and shouts. O'Mara clapped politely and tried to keep the scowl off his face. He had liked the piece fine when Jo and Trevetsky were jumping and kicking, but when they started to dance closer and then get into that sexy stuff, he hadn't liked it one bit. He tried to remember they were dancing roles, but there was something about seeing another man's hands on Jo's body that set him seething. He kept trying to cool himself down, but the more he saw the more he wanted them to stop—and the more he wanted to change places with Trevetsky. How could he feel like this after one dinner and one kiss? It was preposterous. He was cool and smooth; he never got into this kind of a sweat about a woman. Until now. He didn't like it, didn't like the feeling of being out of control.

Sasha and Jo returned to the center of the room and took a bow. "You see how great it is to be a dancer?" Sasha asked. "They pay me to do this with a beautiful woman." He trailed his hand down Jo's arm in a long, sweeping motion. "Not bad, eh?"

"Sasha, darling, do you think I would do it if they didn't pay me?" She pinched his cheek playfully, and he pulled her closer.

"I think you would go all the way to Russia to dance with me, my love." He put his lips dangerously close to hers.

"Nice work if you can get it," Rory commented, and jabbed O'Mara in the ribs.

O'Mara glowered at him. "Isn't it time for us to get out of here?"

"You seemed to be having a good time fifteen minutes ago, buddy."

"That was fifteen minutes ago."

"Mr. O'Mara, Mr. Washington," Jo was saying, "time for the closing bow, gentlemen." The rest of the team was already getting to its feet. "I'm sure you all remember it from last week. Just follow along in the mirror with Sasha and me." He kissed her hand, and she tugged it away gently and signaled the pianist. Fond as she was of her partner, he didn't know when to stop, especially when there was an audience. But that was why he was such a splendid artist—he did nothing by halves.

O'Mara did the bow as perfunctorily as he could and tore out of the room. *Ballet, schmallet,* he thought. *She's just as much a phony as he is.* Halfway down the hall, he stopped dead in his tracks. *Slow down, there, Rory's right. You were having a good time before. Learning something, too. I've got to figure out what it is about her and this ballet stuff that's making me crazy.*

Jo saw O'Mara streak out of the room before the pianist had fully released the last chord of the bow music. The men saw him, too, and their attention was pulled away immediately. They began to murmur to one another, shake their heads and shrug their shoulders. Instead of the class ending on the upbeat note she had expected, the final seconds fell as flat as a pancake.

Just what was going on, she asked herself. One minute he seemed to be enjoying himself; the next he was tearing out of there as if there were a cloud of contagious germs hovering overhead. Maybe he wasn't jealous of Sasha, as she had thought earlier. Maybe she had alienated him by bringing someone into the class who was sure to steal the limelight. No one liked being front and center as much as Sasha did, but J. Fred O'Mara was probably a close contender for the spotlight.

When everyone had left the room, she turned out the lights and locked the door behind her, still puzzling over O'Mara's behavior. She was exasperated. Just as her expectations for successfully teaching the team seemed to be brightening, he had to blow it with one of his displays of temper that were becoming all too familiar to her. She knew he didn't like being forced to be here, especially when he didn't know who was doing the forcing. No one liked to have control of his life taken from his hands, but O'Mara could at least act like a leader and put his personal feelings aside for a couple of hours a week.

Jo set out in the direction of the company dining room. She had an hour before rehearsal and needed to get something to eat. She'd already taken the company class this morning and taught the Empire. Her afternoon would be even busier. Sasha was choreographing his first full-scale ballet for the company's gala opening, and she had the principal role. The music was modern and complex rhythmically, the kind that made her long for the simple one-two-three of a Strauss waltz. The movements and emotions of the piece were equally complex. She reviewed a particularly frustrating passage in her head, marking the steps by approximating them with her hands.

"Where's the orchestra?" a voice boomed out in front of her.

She hadn't seen O'Mara come around the corner. She stopped and looked around in confusion. "What orchestra?"

"The one you were conducting."

She looked down at her hands and began to laugh. She explained to him what she'd been doing, noticing as she spoke how lean and handsome he looked in the jeans and sweatshirt he must have thrown on over his tights and T-shirt. His jacket and athletic bag were slung over one shoulder. "I guess I did look rather strange."

He smiled in recognition. "Yeah, I go over plays in my head all the time. But usually no one catches me at it."

They stood awkwardly for a moment, and Jo made a motion to leave. "Well, I guess I'll see you on Thursday morning."

"Do you have a few minutes?" he asked hurriedly. "It seems that all I ever do is apologize to you, but I wanted to say I was sorry for running out of class like that. It wasn't very bright of me."

"Why did you do it?"

O'Mara hesitated. "All of a sudden I couldn't stand being there. The owner and all," he hedged. He didn't want to lie to her, but he didn't want to make a fool of himself either by telling her why he'd really rushed out. "Listen, do you have time for lunch?"

"I have to be at rehearsal in an hour, but the company dining room is just upstairs."

And Trevetsky is likely to be there, he thought. "Can't we go someplace, um, a bit more private?"

Her pulse took a little leap. "There's a coffee shop a couple of blocks away that makes great hamburgers. I just need to get jeans and a jacket from my locker." She started toward the women's dressing room.

"I thought you dancers were all health-food fanatics," he said when she returned, dressed for the outdoors.

"Some are, but lots more are junk-food fanatics. Mrs. Charles tries to steer us in the right direction. You'd never see a hamburger or, Pavlova preserve us, a French fry in the dining room upstairs. It's all fresh fruit, yogurt and salads."

"It must get boring." He held the door for her, and they stepped out into the bright October sunshine.

"Most of the time I don't think about it. It's convenient, and I have to eat. But every once in a while I wish there was a brownie or a big bowl of fries slathered with ketchup."

He smiled engagingly. "I'd be happy to provide you with both."

"Another time. If I ate that much, I'd never be able to get myself off the ground this afternoon. No, I'll settle for a burger and a glass of milk."

"Then how about if I get the fries and the brownie and look the other way while you steal a couple of bites."

"That sounds like a good plan." As they stepped into Five Brothers Coffee Shop, she was struck by how easily they were getting along. When they had met in the hall neither of them had had time or the chance to put up any fences. With their defenses aside, they could share a conversation as comfortably as a couple of people who'd known each other for a lot longer than they had.

The coffee shop was crowded, but two people were just leaving a small table in the corner. Jo and O'Mara waited until the couple had come down the narrow aisle and then went to claim the table. The waiter cleared away the used dishes and took their order at the same time, since they both knew what they wanted.

"What are you doing this afternoon?" Jo asked.

"Reporting to the stadium for practice, the same as every day during the season."

"At least you have a season. I take a class every day, season or no season."

"What about holidays?"

"There's little enough time for those, but if I do get away for a few days, I make sure to give myself a *barre*."

"A bar of what?" he asked with a grin.

"Chocolate or gold, depending on how I'm feeling at the time," she responded with a grin of her own.

There was a moment of easy silence, and then O'Mara said, "Tell the truth, you never take a day off?"

"Only if I'm so sick I can't move, and that hasn't happened since I caught some terrible stomach bug when we were on tour in the Far East a couple of years ago."

"That must have been fun."

"It most certainly wasn't," Jo said indignantly. "I've never been so miserable in my life."

"Not being sick, the trip."

"Oh," she said with an abashed giggle. The waiter brought their food, and she reached for the ketchup bottle. "There wasn't much time for sight-seeing, but just having been there was an experience." She told him about the trip and then about other tours the company had done in Europe and Latin America. "But you must have plenty of time to travel. All those months off between the end of the season and the start of training."

"That's when I see to my horses," O'Mara said. "Keeping the farm running the way it ought to be run doesn't leave me much time for traveling."

She munched on a French fry, taking small bites to make it last longer. "Who takes care of the place when you're playing? Can't they manage for the time it would take for you to take a vacation?"

"Sure they could. But I don't like leaving the place for as long as I have to now. You see, I want to have a life after football. I don't want to be one of those guys whose years in the pros were the best in his life. I want to be able to move on. I'm laying the groundwork now. It won't be too much longer. Two years, three or four at the outside." He watched her drain her glass of milk, and a thought popped into his head.

His strong reaction to her was starting to make sense. He hadn't realized it consciously until this second, but he was already starting his transition to life on the farm. A wife and kids had always been part of the master plan, but a part he'd never had an urge to act on before. The milk and all its associations must have triggered the connection. He warned himself to be very careful, not to be swayed by the first attractive woman who crossed his path. There was plenty of time to get that side of his life settled.

"How does it feel to be that close to the transition?"
Jo asked. "I wonder about it sometimes, but the end of
my performing days seem so far away—ten, twelve,
maybe fifteen years if I'm incredibly lucky. In a way, I'm
just getting started, just getting to the top."

The waiter served O'Mara's dessert and asked if they
wanted anything else. "Still want to steal a few bites of
brownie?" he asked her.

"Yes, but I don't have time. I'll be late if I don't get
back now." She couldn't believe the hour was already
over. She had expected to look at the clock and see that
she had another fifteen or twenty minutes to spend with
him.

"I'll walk you back." He plucked the brownie from
the plate, took the check from the waiter and on the table left enough to cover it and a tip.

Jo wanted to linger on the way. The sun was warm;
the breeze balmy. Broadway was alive with honking
taxis and noisy buses, with mothers pushing strollers
to the park, music students scurrying by with their
cases, dancers hauling their huge bags full of shoes and
tights and leotards. She wanted a moment to savor the
day, to enjoy it with him, because of him, but she was
conscious of the minutes ticking away. To be late for a
rehearsal was an absolute taboo, especially when Sasha
was running it. He was more demanding about his
choreographic debut than he'd ever been about his
dancing, and that was demanding enough.

They stopped in front of the Metropolitan's door. "I'd
like to see you this weekend," he said, "but we're playing in California. We travel on Saturday, return after
the game on Sunday."

"Another time, then," she said, trying to keep her tone light. They had been thrown into the pot together, and she had thought they'd never mix, like water and oil, but now it seemed their ingredients were more compatible than that. They might cook up quite an agreeable stew together.

"We'll talk about it Thursday."

"All right." They took each other's measure before she turned and disappeared inside the door.

She raced to the dressing room to shuck her jeans and jacket, trying to put the past hour out of her mind. She thought about the section of the ballet she was about to rehearse, but O'Mara kicked the steps right out of her head. On her way to the rehearsal studio, she let the images of him have their way. She'd have to rely on the complex music to clear her crowded, spinning brain.

5

ON SUNDAY MORNING, after taking class with the company, Jo passed up joining her colleagues for their usual session of omelets and gossip. Instead she picked up a bagel and coffee and a hefty *New York Times* and headed home. The Empire's game didn't start till mid-afternoon, but the company's Sunday brunches had been known to last through the afternoon and become Sunday supper, especially on a dreary, rainy day like this one.

As soon as she got home, she dragged her tiny black-and-white portable TV out of the closet and plugged it in. Just to make sure it still worked. She hadn't watched it for weeks. Between her company classes, rehearsals and now teaching the Empire, it was all she could do at night to feed herself, shower and hold a book in front of her face long enough to read two or three pages before she conked out. The snatch of the news program she watched told her the TV was working as badly as ever—fuzzy picture, tinny sound—but it was working. She'd have hated to have to borrow one. Her only close friends were other dancers from the company, and she didn't want to reveal that her interest in the Empire went beyond teaching them to do a proper *plié*.

If it was only football she was interested in, she would have had no trouble calling up Sasha or one of the other football fans in the company and inviting herself to watch the game with him. She was sure she would have added to her meager knowledge of the game if she had. But football was the least of it. It was O'Mara who really had her tuning in.

He'd been a perfect angel in class on Thursday. No outbursts of temper, even when he'd been asked to demonstrate the leaps she had taught the class, not even when the rest of the guys had shortened their usual epithet, Twinkle Toes, to Twink. On the contrary, he seemed to have enjoyed the class from start to finish.

She'd had to rush off immediately after class, so she hadn't gotten a chance to talk to him alone, but she had felt his eyes on her during class, had known he was looking at her for more reason than learning the steps. His awareness of her created an undercurrent of excitement that inspired her teaching. The team's understanding and execution grew not only in their leaps but by leaps and bounds. Whoever the cockamamy owner was and however much O'Mara resented him, his scheme might turn out to have bigger and better results than he had imagined.

To pass the time before the game, Jo brewed a pot of coffee, ate her bagel and had a leisurely look at the newspaper. Then she had a long soak in the tub, washed her hair, rinsed out a few tights and leotards and did her nails. Fresh and relaxed, comfortably dressed in a bright coral sweat suit, she curled up on the couch to watch the game.

The Rattlers won the toss and proceeded to break through the Empire defense with ease. Two first downs later, the Rattlers were within fifteen yards of scoring. It was beginning to look as if the Empire were in for another rout. Between plays, a camera picked up the Empire sideline, and she caught a glimpse of O'Mara stalking up and down, shouting at the men on the field. From the expression on his face, she thought there was a good possibility his words would have been bleeped out even if a microphone had picked them up. But to her and everyone in the stadium's surprise, the Empire managed not only to hold off the Rattlers but also to gain possession of the ball.

O'Mara led the offense onto the field, clapping the men on the back or the bottom as they raced to the line of scrimmage. They gained more than twenty yards in the next couple of plays, and Jo found herself pounding the sofa in excitement. O'Mara tried a pass next. She watched him go back, aim and hurl the ball at Rory. She watched Rory advance on the ball and extend his arms for it. She watched a Rattler intercept the pass at the last second. She stopped pounding the sofa and let out a king-size sigh.

The ball changed hands so many times in the rest of the first half that she lost count. Every time the Empire rallied, they lost control of the ball before they could score. But at least, she told herself, they were rallying. And they had kept the Rattlers from getting on the scoreboard. The way they were playing seemed to her untutored eye a big improvement over the game she'd watched from the owner's box the previous Sunday.

While the half-time show was on she went into the kitchen to pop a bowl of popcorn. She was shaking the pan over the gas, marking some steps from the Stravinsky ballet she would be rehearsing in the morning, when she heard O'Mara's voice. She turned off the gas and dashed into the living room.

The interview had obviously been recorded before the game. O'Mara, in neat slacks and an open-collared sport shirt, sat with the commentator. He was composed, at ease, confident, good-humored and remained that way even when the interviewer made some sharp digs about the Empire's capabilities. The only time he showed a hint of temper was when he was asked about the identity of the Empire's owner. His hands tightened on the arms of his chair, and his face tensed. "I have nothing to say on that subject," he told the interviewer with a look that warned the man to change the subject if he knew what was good for him. The interviewer retreated, and O'Mara resumed his bantering tone.

As she watched the rest of the interview, Jo considered what was happening between her and O'Mara. They'd had their clashes, that was certain, but that there was a connection between them that couldn't be denied. Nor did she want to deny it. So what if he had a touchy temper and a tendency to forget his manners? He was terrific looking, sexy, forceful, and somewhere under all those muscles there was a strong heart and a sensitive soul. She had begun to get a glimpse of that when they'd had lunch together. Now she admitted to herself that she wanted to have a much closer look at the real J. Fred O'Mara.

She realized that a shaving-cream commercial had come on and went back to her popcorn. She munched it compulsively during the tense third quarter. The Empire missed scoring by only a few yards, not once but three times in the fifteen minutes. The calls were so close that loyalties were divided among the fans. They roared for the home team, but the Empire were such underdogs that the crowd was cheering them on', too. Jo knew the team couldn't hear her, but she rooted and chanted along, with the people in the stands.

With less than five minutes remaining in the fourth quarter, it looked as though the game was going to go into overtime. O'Mara had pressed the Empire to within ten yards of the goal, but the Rattlers line was determined to hold them back. At fourth down with three to go, O'Mara called time and huddled with the team. They broke up with a shout and re-formed on the line. The ball was put into play, and it looked as if O'Mara was going to pass. He took two steps back and looked for his receiver. The Rattler defense was aiming "sack the quarterback," bring O'Mara down and steal the ball. A man had gone down in front of him, and he was blocked on both sides so that he couldn't go forward. Jo shouted for O'Mara to get rid of the ball. But none of his receivers were in a good position.

She could hardly believe what she saw next. O'Mara tucked the ball under his arm and leaped. Not only did he leap, he went into the jump with the running steps of the *grand jeté*. He bent his knees in the two preparatory steps, sprang into the air, cleared the downed player and landed—knees bent as she had taught—with a clear straightaway to the goal line. He raced down the field and between the posts. The umpire blew his whistle and raised his arms. O'Mara threw down the ball, and the Empire converged on him, hugging him and each other and jumping up and down joyfully. The team had scored its first touchdown of the season.

Jo hugged herself and jumped up and down. "I helped with that," she said out loud with joy and disbelief. "Me, Jo Sherbourne. All five-foot-four, one hundred five pounds of me." She collapsed onto the couch in a near swoon.

THE NEXT DAY Jo felt as light as a feather, as strong as an ox. Her kicks were higher, straighter than ever before, her footwork sharper; her turns could have been executed on a dime. Several of the company members commented that she was in exceptional form and wanted to know what she had been eating or drinking or doing to have attained such an effect. Jo merely smiled and shrugged.

She hardly felt tired when she left for home that evening and stifled several urges to dance down the street. She had started up the stoop when Carlos, the superintendent who lived in the ground-floor apartment, stuck his head out his window to tell her he had a package for her.

"You got a new boyfriend or something?" he asked as he came out the wrought-iron door at street level that led to his apartment. He handed her a large box wrapped in silver foil paper and tied with a huge red bow. "This looks pretty fancy."

Part of Carlos's job—as he defined it—was to keep up with the personal lives of all his tenants. To him that was as important as taking out the trash and keeping the halls and stairways clean.

"Yes, it does," Jo said evasively. She masked her excitement, thanked a disappointed Carlos and continued up the stoop. She could hardly wait to climb to the second floor, open her door and rip off the paper. The second she'd closed her door behind her, she dropped her carry sack on the floor and started to tear at the ribbon. She stopped herself abruptly. *This isn't the way to do this,* she scolded herself. She made herself pick up her bag, hang up her coat and sit down on the sofa before starting again to carefully undo the ribbon and slip off the paper.

A small white envelope was taped to the top of the box, on which there was another layer of silver paper. She opened the envelope and pulled out two pieces of paper. One was a ticket to the Empire's home game the following Sunday; the other was a pass that would admit her to the players' lounge after the game. She reached inside the envelope to see if there was a card or note, but it was empty.

Maybe there was something inside the box itself. She took off the wrapping, and for a moment forgot about finding an enclosure card. She was staring at a two-pound box of her favorite chocolate truffles. Temptation and heaven itself in her hands. A form of signature so clear that no card was needed. No one but her closest friends and family—and J. Fred O'Mara—knew of her weakness for chocolate truffles. What a lovely romantic gesture, she thought as she sank her teeth into a creamy candy. She ate a second and then closed the box. She'd dole them out to herself over the week. It might make the week go faster.

She didn't say anything to O'Mara at either class about the candy or the ticket, and he didn't say anything to her. During the classes she often caught him looking at her in the mirror, and found her attention straying to him more times than he warranted as a pupil, even though once again he picked up the turns she was teaching faster than anyone in the class, even Rory. The looks that passed between them were warm, speculative, electric, and sometimes flustered when they were surprised in the act of sizing each other up. They chatted briefly after each class, about the Empire's first victory, about the progress the team was making in class. What they said was of little importance; what was, was the measure they took of each other, the mental notes they were taking.

This week has been good, Jo thought as she scurried off to grab a bite of lunch after teaching the class of Thursday. *We've kept our distance, avoided clashes, taken a better look at each other.* She felt strong and eager, more excited about O'Mara and the possibilities of him than she had about anything since Sasha had asked her to dance the principal role in his debut ballet.

After class Sunday, Jo dressed carefully in a clinging royal-blue jersey dress with a calf-length skirt, then cinched it with a low-slung calf-leather belt in hot pink. Her hair she left loose. Since she was going to the game alone and she didn't want to take the long subway ride to the stadium in Queens, she'd booked a car service to pick her up at her apartment and take her to the game. Ready a full fifteen minutes before her car was due, she sat on the edge of the couch to wait for it. She'd been anticipating the game all week and so was surprised at how calm and composed she felt, excited but not at all nervous or jittery. She thoroughly enjoyed eating the last truffle in the box, which she'd saved for precisely this moment, thinking it would help distract her from her nerves. The truffle tasted even better since she had no nerves to distract her.

Though the car that arrived was only an ordinary sedan, Jo, wrapped up in a long Missoni sweater coat for warmth, felt as regal and privileged sitting in the back seat as she would have in a stretch limousine. She turned a few heads when the driver helped her out of the car at the stadium's main gate and a few more as she walked to the entrance gate inside. The attention made her step springier, her posture jauntier. She took her seat at the fifty-yard line, only one tier above the owner's box, with as much assurance as someone who owned a lifetime subscription to it.

Watching the game from the stands was more exciting than watching it from the owner's box. She felt like part of the crowd out here, felt the strong, dogged loyalty that the fans had for a team with the worst record in professional football, felt the surging spirit that had been fired by the Empire's upset victory over the Rattlers the previous weekend. She drank a beer and ate a hot dog and cheered and yelled, drawing curious looks from those around her, both because she was a beautiful woman alone and because she called all the players by name in her exhortations.

The game was another close one. The Atlanta team began it with the supposition that the Empire's defeat of the Rattlers had been a fluke. But the men soon realized that the Keystone Kops of pro football had been busy turning themselves into an adequate if not a crack force. Atlanta had to work hard to keep the Empire from scoring and to prevent their own offense from being thwarted on every play. As in the previous Empire game, there was no score at the end of the third quarter.

With three minutes left on the clock, the Empire regained possession of the ball on its own ten-yard line. They had three minutes to make ninety yards. That seemed impossible, even if they could retain possession of the ball, for which they had struggled throughout the game. O'Mara made up twenty yards on a fine pass. On the second play, Atlanta stopped him with only inches gained. On the third play, they misjudged the Empire's strategy. O'Mara skirted their line and had a clear corridor to the goalposts. He put his head down and began to run. The crowd was euphoric and began to scream. Jo took her eyes off him for a split second and noticed an Atlanta tackle bearing down on him. "Watch out!" she yelled, but her voice disappeared into the cacophony. She tried telegraphing the thought to O'Mara.

Just then he looked behind him and saw that he was being chased. But he seemed to slow down instead of speed up. The tackle was within inches of him and reached out to dive for O'Mara. It looked as if O'Mara would go down, but the instant before the tackle's hands made contact with his legs, O'Mara took a preparatory step and whirled around on one foot. The tackle thudded to the ground, chin first; O'Mara scrambled for the end zone.

A pirouette! Jo was elated as she clapped and jumped up and down with the rest of the crowd. He'd done a pirouette! She was nearly delirious by the time the referees put the ball back into play after the touchdown. The final minutes were played out swiftly, and the Empire took their second victory. It was an astonishing, unbelievable turnabout for the team.

The final whistle signaled pandemonium in the stadium, and Jo joined in. The fans cheered and whooped until they were hoarse. While the stadium quieted down and people filed out, she slid into her seat to recover. The place was nearly empty before she felt steady enough to ask an usher for directions to the players' lounge.

The pandemonium in the lounge was greater than it had been outside as friends and family gathered to wait for the players to emerge from the locker room. In the stadium the jubilation had been released into the open air; in the lounge the force was contained and seemed sufficient to launch a rocket. Champagne flowed freely. Jo accepted a glass as well as a joyous hug from the server.

She stood aside as she sipped her sparkling wine, surveying the room with a curious mixture of detachment and involvement. More than a couple of people glanced in her direction and whispered among themselves, but that didn't bother her at all. In fact she liked being the "mystery woman"; it sharpened her already well-honed exhilaration.

O'Mara was the first player to enter the room. A loud cheer went up when he burst through the door. He was obviously fresh from the shower, his dark hair still damp and clinging to his head, his face still pink from exertion, hot water and a close shave. A waiter near the door thrust a glass of champagne into his hand, but he thrust it back, grabbing the bottle and guzzling directly from it. The room went wild with laughter and cheering, and Jo clapped her hands in delight.

O'Mara put the bottle down on the tray and started into the room, shaking hands, accepting and giving claps on the back as he passed. Jo didn't move toward him but stayed stock-still, eyes trained on him, waiting for him to notice her. He stopped short when he did, looked at her keenly and immediately moved toward her, brushing aside any other congratulatory handshakes or back claps that would have slowed him down.

He held out both hands to her and beamed at her. "Jo," he said quietly as he put her hands in his.

"Congratulations," she said.

He was surprised and pleased beyond belief to see her. She must really care about the team, maybe even about him, if she'd bothered to make her way here today. Tickets to Empire games were easy enough to come by; although they sold more tickets than most losing teams, there were always plenty of empty seats. He did, however, wonder briefly how she'd gotten a pass to the lounge. She must have asked the ballet school lady, Mrs. Robert—no, Charles—to set one up. Really he didn't care how she'd gotten here; he was tickled that she had. "Not a bad turn of events, eh?" He squeezed her hands and moved closer to her.

"Not too bad." She knew from the sudden hush in the room that they had an audience, but it didn't matter. They were making their own private room with their eyes.

"You look wonderful." In tights and leotards, her hair pinned securely to her head, she was beautiful, but in "civilian" clothes she was ravishing. Her long, loose hair was glorious, her lean body more womanly, more desirable with more clothes on it than less.

"Thank you."

Other team members began to filter into the room, and the merrymaking resumed. Several people crowded around them, and politeness demanded that O'Mara make introductions. He told people only her name, nothing about her, especially that Jo was the team's ballet teacher. The news was not public yet, and even though the Empire had started winning, Jo didn't think he would want the press jumping all over them and making connections between the ballet classes and their two-game streak. Especially since the dance training had been foisted on him and the team by the much-resented, anonymous owner. Since the worlds of dance and football rarely overlapped, no one recognized her. Some of the players' wives must have realized who she was, but none of them risked arguments with their husbands by spilling the beans.

The impromptu party continued into early evening, and Jo had a simply wonderful time. Her life had revolved around dancing for so long that she rarely socialized with people who weren't involved in some way in her own small world. She'd been Jo Sherbourne, ballerina, since adolescence; it was refreshing and energizing to be plain Jo Sherbourne for a few hours.

When the crowd had begun to thin out O'Mara took her aside, hoping she didn't already have plans for the evening. She seemed to have come to the game alone and didn't know anyone but the players. "What would you say to joining me for dinner?"

"Yes," she answered simply. Although his invitation hadn't mentioned dinner, she had assumed he would want to spend the evening with her, so having him ask her to dinner seemed slightly strange. But she was glad to see he wasn't taking anything for granted. A change of scenery would be welcome, too. She was feeling heady from the champagne and the noise and excitement. The gathering was fun, but it was hardly the romantic date the truffles had presaged.

"Someplace quiet," he suggested, as if reading her mind.

She nodded her agreement.

It took a quarter of an hour for the remaining revelers to let O'Mara take his leave, but Jo and O'Mara finally made their way out of the players' lounge to his reserved parking space. He handed her into the Jag, and at last they were alone, side by side, speeding toward Manhattan.

6

WHEN O'MARA SAID QUIET he meant it. The place he took her to was tucked away in the West Village, on the ground floor of one of the old-style tenement buildings just a block or two from the Hudson River. Half of the ten tables were empty; the other diners were speaking so softly that the two could hear sizzling sounds as they passed the kitchen. A waiter seated them at a table next to one of the exposed brick walls and propped up a blackboard menu on a spare chair.

Jo hadn't expected to be taken anyplace so unpretentious as this neighborhood bistro. She'd expected O'Mara to show off a bit more but was very glad he hadn't. "This is really nice," she said. "I don't get downtown very often."

"With your schedule you probably don't get anywhere very often."

"You're right."

"Why do you do it?"

No one had asked her that for years. In high school her friends hadn't understood how she could take the train into the city every afternoon after school, do her homework on the way, take four hours of dance classes, return home at nine o'clock, eat dinner and get up and do it all again the next day. She had tried to explain it to them, but the dedication she had come to so early had little meaning. "Because I love it. Because it's all I know, all I've ever wanted. Don't you feel that way about what you do?"

"Hell, no," O'Mara said with a broad grin. "Football's an accident. I found out I could play. It got me through college, and it's made me a wealthy man. I'm looking forward to the day I retire."

"How can you do something so well if you don't like it? It's not as if it's an easy sport to play. You guys get as knocked around as we do."

"I didn't say I didn't like it. I don't have a passion for it."

"But how can you give the best years of your life to something you're not passionately involved in?"

The waiter came back and asked them if they'd like drinks or wine. O'Mara suggested a carafe of the house red, and Jo agreed. The waiter returned immediately with it.

"What shall we drink to?" O'Mara asked as he filled their glasses.

"The Empire's finest era," she offered, and raised her glass to his. The wine was rough and unsophisticated, the kind of wine she'd had often when the company was on tour in France. She settled into her chair, very glad he hadn't taken her to someplace fancy where he would have been recognized, where there would have been a long wine list and a longer menu.

"And to a closer collaboration between sport and art," he said when they'd drunk the first toast.

His tone was light, as if he were only talking about her teaching the team. But the unspoken personal message was clear. Her hand was slightly unsteady as she raised her glass a second time. He held her eyes as they drank. She took too large a sip, and the wine burned her throat on the way down, but she welcomed it to ward off the chill his look had sent down her spine. "You never answered my question," she said, peeling her eyes away from his.

"I've forgotten what it was. I was thinking about something else."

Jo was too shaken to follow the path his answer pointed to. "I asked how you could give your best years to something you have no passion for."

"Who said these are my best years? Even with an average life expectancy, I haven't reached the halfway mark yet." He leaned closer and said in a low, conspiratorial voice, "You ain't seen nuttin' yet, honey."

Jo had to laugh at his delivery and couldn't resist mimicking it. "Oh, yeah? Whatcha got in mind?" He reached across the table and ran a finger lightly over the back of hers. She got that shivery feeling again and had to fight against withdrawing her hand from his.

"The best horse farm in the whole country. Horses that will sire generations. Horses that will be remembered long after J. Fred O'Mara is only a footnote in the football record books. It takes money to start that kind of farm and run it right. I wasn't born with any dough, so I had to come up with it somehow. Luckily I play a mean game of football."

"That you do," she said quietly. If he had planned this evening minute by minute, he couldn't have done better. She was having such a good time talking to him, learning about him. How could she ever have thought he was a clumsy cad? Looking back, she could now see the funny side of their encounter in the owner's private box. She wasn't aware of smiling, but he asked to be let in on the joke. She told him what she was thinking about.

They began to relive the evening moment by moment. The more they remembered the funnier it became. The laughter that followed left them breathless. They stopped short of remembering the ride home and O'Mara's sudden kiss on her doorstep. But they both knew what was on the other's mind.

"Shall we order?" O'Mara said when they had quieted down. "I'm getting awfully hungry." His eyes devoured her as he said it.

"Me, too," she said. She wasn't used to saying things that could be taken two ways. But her response was as loaded as his question. He knew it; she knew it. The innuendo made her feel daring, even more aware of him.

They nibbled on a slice of pâté and rounds of crusty French bread while they waited for their steaks, *pommes frites* and salads. O'Mara described his farm for her—the land, the buildings, the horses, his plans. Hearing him talk about it made her feel unaccountably jealous. She told him so.

"Why?" he asked.

"I don't know." She sipped at her wine and thought. "Maybe because it makes me realize how much of the world I've closed off as a dancer. Look at me. It's a big deal to come downtown for dinner."

"It is for me, too, with you."

"That's very flattering, but you're changing the subject."

"Everyone has to walk their own path, Jo. Yours is narrow and straight; other people have curves and hills. We can't walk anyone else's. No one would ever get where they were going."

"What a wonderful way of thinking about life," she said admiringly.

"Us dumb jocks occasionally come up with a good line or two."

She looked down at the table. She didn't like to be reminded that she had assumed he was a "dumb jock" just because he played football. He reached out and lifted her chin. "You're not taking that remark personally, are you?" She nodded. "We can't have that. I know you've changed your mind about me."

"Oh, really?"

"Except you still think I'm an arrogant son of a—"

"That'll do," she put in quickly.

"Are we friends?"

"We're getting there."

Over the meal O'Mara asked question after question. She told him about growing up in a suburban town north of New York City, about auditioning for and being accepted at the Metropolitan Ballet School when she was fourteen, about joining the company right after high school graduation, about her years in the corps, her rise to soloist and now the principal dancer. She found it easy to talk to him. He drew her out gently, laughed at her funny stories, commiserated when she told him about the rocky parts of the road she'd traveled.

By the time the waiter cleared their plates, she'd talked about everything significant about her career except her partnership with Sasha. O'Mara didn't ask about it, so she didn't volunteer any information. There was more than a touch of green in his blue eyes, she had discovered at close range. She didn't want to do anything to bring it out. Not when the evening was proceeding without so much as a hiccup.

They took their time over dessert and coffee. She got O'Mara to do his share of the talking by asking him to explain to her some of the finer points of football. She thought it would help her in her teaching to know such things as the function of each player, how plays and strategy were planned. He answered her questions patiently and thoroughly and used a lot of humorous anecdotes to make his points. She had asked out of curiosity about him and a sense of duty about her work, but she ended up laughing as she learned.

"I guess it's the effect of winning," O'Mara said as they walked to his car, "but I've still got energy to burn. Would you like to go dancing?"

"Dancing?" she answered with a laugh. "Talk about a busman's holiday."

"I didn't mean you should whip out your toe shoes. I was thinking about stopping in at Neptune."

"Isn't that a disco?"

He looked at her incredulously. "You really do walk the straight and narrow, don't you? Neptune is not *a* disco, it's *the* dance club."

"What are we waiting for?"

O'Mara helped her into the Jag and watched her fold her legs gracefully into the low body of the car. He'd always believed that ballet dancers had ugly, muscular legs, but in those dark stockings and sleek boots her legs looked anything but ugly and muscular. In fact, no matter what she wore, they were as terrific as the rest of her, which was terrific enough. He couldn't remember having had a better time with a woman. She was bright, funny, beautiful, and he loved the way her face showed every tiny change of mood and feeling. She wasn't coy, wasn't with him because she was impressed by his status and money. He like that about her. He'd had far too much of the other since he'd become a rich and famous quarterback.

He closed the car door carefully and fairly danced around to the other side. He was so glad she'd shown up this afternoon, and he was more than a bit miffed at himself for not thinking of getting her a ticket and a pass to the lounge. But one of his mares had gotten sick this week, and there had been extra hours in the Empire game room, and then he'd spent all that time sweet talking Patti Pringle about doing some investigative journalism into who the owner really was. Of course, Patti wanted something in return. He'd almost put her on to the story of the team taking ballet lessons but had decided to save it. The longer it was a secret the more it would be worth.

He got back into the car and once more turned his attention to Jo. "Are you sure going to a club won't ruin your form?" He certainly wouldn't want to be responsible for ruining a form like hers.

"Heck, no," she said, patting her stomach. Only she would notice the slight bulge there, but the hearty meal had produced one. "It'll help me work off some of the *pommes frites*. When you stand on your toes for hours with only some cardboard and satin for support, you notice every ounce."

"Is that all that's in those shoes? Cardboard and satin?" he asked incredulously.

"There are steel shanks on the bottoms of the shoes to prevent them from collapsing, but what we stand on is basically several layers of cardboard and glue, covered with satin. We also pack our toes with lamb's wool, but that's to prevent rubbing inside the shoe. It doesn't offer any support."

O'Mara let out a low whistle. "That sounds to me like the equivalent of playing with a cardboard helmet. I know I don't stand on my head during a game, but sometimes the opposing team stands on it for me. I'm glad I get to protect my body better than you do."

Jo laughed at the thought of dressing like a football player to dance. "Can you see me trying to dance wearing shoulder pads and hard plastic toe shoes? I wouldn't be able to balance or turn or jump. I'm amazed that you can move as well as you do in all that armor."

"Frankly, so am I sometimes. But all you have to do is get one cleat in your thigh to know how important the padding is. Still, we get around pretty well, don't we?"

"You're certainly improving. Even a football illiterate like me knows that. You did a wonderful pirouette out there on the field today. It sure fooled that tackle."

He looked at her sharply. "What pirouette? What are you talking about?" She recounted his movements on the field during that play, step by step. "Believe me, it was entirely unintentional," he protested. "I wasn't thinking about pirouettes. I was thinking about getting away from that guy."

"Ah, that's just it. Your muscles knew what to do. You didn't have to think about it."

"So you think the ballet is helping?" he asked thoughtfully.

"Have you been winning or losing since you started?"

"It could be just a coincidence." The team was coming together, but if ballet had anything to do with it, he was sure it was only because being forced into the experience had given the guys something to share, a kind of solidarity.

"It could be," she allowed. "Are you doing anything else different in training?"

"No, just more of it."

"I rest my case."

"So you really think I did a pirouette out there today?"

"And a leap over a pile of men last Sunday." She recapped that play step by step, as well.

"I'm still not convinced, but you've got an incredible memory for what went on during a play, especially since you don't know much about football."

"Training, O'Mara. How do you think I remember the scores of ballets I dance?"

"Hey, you called me O'Mara, not Fr—that other name." He paused and reached for her hand. "Thanks," he said, giving her a squeeze. "I hate being called that."

"You're welcome. Maybe sometime you'll tell me why you dislike 'that other name' so much."

"Sometime," he said softly, "when we're alone and very close. So no one else will hear."

The thought of being alone and close to him, sharing a secret, put a large lump smack in the middle of Jo's throat. She swallowed hard.

O'Mara pulled the car to a stop. Jo looked out the window and found herself in unfamiliar territory. "Where are we?" There were rows of warehouses on either side of the avenue, all dark and deserted.

"Twelfth Avenue in the Fifties. Neptune is just around the corner."

The block they turned into when they got out of the car looked as unpromising as the one where they'd parked. As they walked down the street, Jo noticed an unusual number of expensive cars lining the curbs. Toward the middle of the block the sidewalks were overflowing with people. "Are all these people waiting to get in?" Of course she'd heard about the crowds that waited to get into hot night spots but had never seen one. The scene struck her as a cross between a parade route and a vigil. The festive air was overlaid with one of anxiety and concern.

O'Mara piloted her through the sea of people. "Don't worry. We won't have to wait. Being a star quarterback has it advantages."

That it did. O'Mara signaled to the doorkeeper, and immediately two burly men stepped into the street and created an aisle for them to walk through. As they passed Jo heard shouts of "Who's that?" and "Who are they?" O'Mara was identified quickly and easily, but there were no balletomanes near the head of the Neptune line that night. Jo had never thirsted for stardom, didn't need it the way some dancers, Sasha for instance, needed it. But she found herself listening closely to the crowd, waiting to hear if someone had recognized her. No one did, and she felt slighted. She was near the top of her public, glamorous profession, and still no one recognized her on the street. Her feelings were occasioned by more than being with O'Mara. For a long time she'd been content to stay in the shadows, to be a member of the company rather than a prima ballerina. Perhaps she was more ready than she had realized to make a move into the limelight.

Several people waved and shouted to O'Mara. Two or three held out pens and papers for autographs. He smiled and saluted his admirers, but he and Jo were whisked inside the door by the bouncers before he could stop to sign his name for anyone.

"Great game today," one of the bouncers complimented him.

O'Mara reached inside his sport jacket and pulled out a couple of tickets. "Thanks. Come see the next home game." He thrust the tickets into the man's hand.

The man grinned and took them. "Keep playing the way you did today, and you won't have so many of these to give away."

"I hope not," O'Mara responded heartily. Hand at the small of Jo's back, he guided her into the reception area.

"Do you always carry around spare tickets?" she asked, raising her voice over the din of loud, throbbing music.

"You never know when they'll come in handy."

"I can't imagine carrying around free tickets to the ballet. I don't expect I'd find many takers here."

"You'd be surprised. People will take anything if it's free."

"Thanks," she said wryly.

"I didn't mean that the way it sounded. I just meant that more people than you think would be willing to give going to the ballet a try."

"Ever been to one yourself, O'Mara?"

"No," he admitted.

"Remind me to send you a ticket to opening night. Turnabout is fair play."

"What did you say?" he yelled. The music seemed to have been thrown up another ten decibels.

"I said—" she began.

"Tell me later." He hooked his arm through hers. "Let's get a table and then dance. There's no use trying to talk in here."

He led her to the entrance of the dance floor, where they waited for one of the silver-jacketed hosts to find them a table. The scene made Jo think they were about to enter a great underwater chamber. The insistent, infectious music unleashed enormous, undulating tides of energy into the room, and everything in it—animate and inanimate—moved to its beat. Greenish-blue lighting heightened the effect of being submerged in sound and motion.

O'Mara's body bounced easily in time to the music as they followed the host through the dense maze of tables to one on the edge of the dance floor. Although the rhythm couldn't have been more plain, Jo's body resisted it. Years of disciplined training had given her a control of her body that was second nature. She tried but couldn't shed it as if it were a too-warm coat.

"Ringside seats," he shouted to her as they squeezed into the two small chairs beside a tiny table.

A waitress in a skin-tight red lamé jumpsuit, distinguishable from the rest of the crowd only by her tray, came to take their drink order. How she heard what they said to her was a mystery to Jo, but she nodded and danced off to answer the waves of the people a couple of tables away, who looked as if they had worked up a powerful thirst.

O'Mara leaned across the table and took her arm. "Let's dance!" he yelled. "You can show them all how it's supposed to be done."

"I don't think so," she replied. "I'm not used to making it up as I go along."

He shrugged out of his sport jacket and draped it over the back of the chair. "It's easy. Take it from a pro," he said as he helped her out of her chair.

O'Mara took the dance floor with the same ease that he took the field for the first offensive play of a game. The music was fast with a Latin beat, and in seconds he was moving hands, feet, shoulders, hips in perfect synch. His joints moved as if they'd been newly oiled. Jo gaped at him; the stiffness he exhibited in ballet class had disappeared. He whirled around rapidly and caught her by the arm.

"What are you waiting for?" He didn't miss a beat or stop moving.

"Inspiration!" she shouted back. "What do I do?"

"Whatever the music tells you." He let go of her arm and executed a series of fast two-step turns.

All around her there were gyrating bodies, no two of them doing the same thing at the same time. She felt awkward as she picked up the beat and began to move, though not because she was worried she'd do something "wrong," as a self-conscious person might. This dancing was all whimsy, created in the heat of the moment; the steps were never meant to be repeated. Her awkwardness stemmed from having spent twenty of her twenty-eight years learning to move gracefully, using her body as a single, fluid unit. She had never broken her body into its component parts as the dancers here were doing. She tried to mimic their movements but couldn't get the hang of simultaneously thrusting her hips from side to side, moving her feet to the pounding beat and shaking her shoulders.

"Pretend you're a rag doll," O'Mara said as he stepped in close to her.

She tried letting herself go limp and was starting to loosen up when suddenly a new record came over the sound system. Everyone around her switched over to the new beat without taking a breath, but she was still moving to the Latin rhythm. It took her a moment to catch up, but then she was stiff again. She sidled up to O'Mara. "This feels weird."

"You can't feel as weird as I do in tights trying to dance to Chopin." He circled around her, bending at the knees to bring his face close to hers.

Something about the look he gave her prodded her into a spontaneous countercircle around him. She turned her back to his and looked over one shoulder to see his face. He suddenly reversed the direction, and she followed with only a slight hesitation.

"All right!" he complimented, and flashed her a brilliant smile.

"I think I'm starting to get it," she mumbled, concentrating on keeping the momentum going.

He moved back and away from her and began a series of intricate hand and shoulder movements. She kept her eye on him, and translated his moves to her feet and hips. Her ever-straight spine was beginning to loosen up. The feeling was so strange it sent a shiver through her whole body. Her head, arms and shoulders shook in response to it. The unexpected motion gave her a sudden sense that her body had learned the trick of disco dancing. She was moving all her separate parts now but not mechanically. She felt the connections between them in a new and different way.

O'Mara danced closer, leaned forward and put his hands on her shoulders. "That's it. You're getting as loose as a goose."

"I just hope I don't honk." They laughed together, and he bent down to touch his forehead to hers. The moment, intimate and exuberant at once, surprised her. She reached out to him and put her hands on his waist. They invented a skipping step that evolved into a series of jitterbug-style turns, with O'Mara twisting her over and under his arm.

They danced on until they were breathless, which took a long time for their well-trained bodies. When they returned to their table they found their drinks, ice half-melted, cocktail napkins under the glasses soaked through. They didn't try to talk above the music as they sipped the cool liquid, and though they were seated, the music still charged their inner rhythms.

After a few minutes' rest, Jo began to tap out the beat on the table with a single finger. O'Mara joined her but used both hands. She put her other hand into motion, and soon they were having a hand dance with each other. Their hands reached across the table, touched and parted, twined and untwined, teased and retreated. They giggled as their hands jumped and leaped, turned up and down, in and out. They grew as breathless as they had on the dance floor, but this time it was not from exertion. It was from touching and being touched by each other. Their hand dance continued, in time with the music, but it was less frenetic, more fanciful. The movement around them faded into the background; they could have been alone in a small room with a stereo playing softly. Their eyes locked and held; their breaths quickened further.

The music changed abruptly; the lights flickered and dimmed. The loud thrumming base beat disappeared, and the slow wail of a female singer on the tape took over. O'Mara lightly took her hands and tugged at them. They rose together and moved onto the dance floor.

He wrapped her in his arms and held her close. She felt this music more deeply than all the throbbing, fast records they had danced to combined. The singer's voice seemed to burrow into her brain and send its longing, aching, yearning shooting through her body. She shuddered, and his arms tightened around her. He kissed the top of her head and rested his cheek on the warm spot. The weight of him, the solidness of him should have anchored her to the floor, but she felt as if she were floating, drifting on a beautiful blue-green sea.

Their movements in this dance were as slow, as measured as they had been rapid and impromptu in the first round of dances. And Jo had no trouble getting the hang of dancing like this with O'Mara. She felt more graceful, more lyrical, more lovely than she ever had in any of the hundreds of *pas de deux* danced in her career. There was a delight in this movement that had little to do with the body; it went beyond that, to the heart and the soul.

The last plaintive note of the song sounded, but it didn't fade away. The disc jockey pushed it away with another pulsing vibrating beat. O'Mara didn't let her go. They held on to each other, on to the feeling of the dance, the memory of the music.

"Let's get out of here," he said. He moved to her side, put his arm around her shoulder and piloted her off the dance floor. On the way through the packed tables, he stopped their waitress and put a folded bill into her hand.

Jo barely breathed until they were outside. Their hour inside hadn't diminished the crowd in the street. O'Mara put his head down and skirted it quickly, ignoring the calls of those who recognized him. He seemed as determined as she to hold on to the magical time under the swimming sea-green lights of Neptune.

He didn't speak until after they'd reached the car and pulled away from the curb. "May I take you home?" He sounded formal, as if he might be protecting himself from a refusal. He was asking for far more than to take her to her door. He would expect to come through it and not emerge until morning.

"I'd like you to," she replied. His formality was contagious, and she liked him all the more for asking in the way he had. They were about to take a giant step together. She was glad to see that he—like she—hadn't taken it for granted that they would spend the night together.

"Good," he said, and smiled very tenderly at her.

At the door to her building, her hand trembled as she drew the key from her purse. She dropped it, and he bent gallantly to pick it up. He gave her the key, brushing her hand as he placed it in her palm. She laughed lightly to cover her nerves, her excitement, and slipped the key into the lock.

The door to her apartment was just inside the vestibule, on the right side of the hall. He rested his hand on her shoulder as she unlocked both the locks and opened the door. "Please come in," she said, and stepped inside to flick on a light.

"Thank you." O'Mara took a moment to look around the room. The architectural details of what had once been the front parlor of the brownstone had been well-preserved. The carved plaster of the fireplace was intact, as was that in the ceiling moldings. The oak parquet floors were burnished with age but gleamed with polish. She had added little to the room—a plum-colored Victorian sofa, a small antique Persian rug under the coffee table, two Oriental prints over the mantel. The place was as streamlined, as uncluttered as Jo herself. "You have a lovely home."

"Thank you," she said, genuinely pleased. "I always think other people will find it bare. But it suits me."

"Yes, it does. It's very much like you." He turned to her and brought her closer. "That's why I like it so much."

He grinned, and the formality disappeared. The hardest moment, the threshold had been crossed. "Would you like some coffee?" she asked comfortably. She put her purse on the small table in the dining alcove and dropped her wrap over the back of a chair.

"No, thanks," he said, removing his sport jacket and placing it on top of hers on the chair. "But I could use another dance. Just like the last one. That was nice. Real nice," he drawled in a low, throaty voice.

"Dancing I can supply. Music is another matter. I'm not sure my stereo would know how to play music like we heard at Neptune—even if I had any. There's always the radio—"

He silenced her with a finger over her lips. "We'll make our own music. That way we won't wake the neighbors." His finger trailed over her chin, down her throat and through the cleft between her breasts. Both arms circled her shoulders and drew her to him.

Without the distractions of music and atmospheric lights and other people, she was so much more aware of him. The softness of his linen shirt against her cheek, the tapering lines of his back, the rock-hard tautness of the muscles in his back and thighs. Softly he hummed a tuneless song as he guided her slowly around the small space between the dining alcove and living room. She felt it more than heard it. It tickled her ear, her neck, the curve of her shoulder. She laughed, almost soundlessly, from the pure joy of being held by him.

He stopped moving for a moment and covered her mouth with his. He tasted warm and sweet, and she rose to her toes to get closer to him. He responded to her move instantly, welding his lips harder, more fervently to hers. One hand went to the small of her back; the other supported the middle of her back as he kissed her more and more passionately. His tongue licked at her lips, snuggled in between them, explored the warm, dark corners of her mouth. He pressed down on her, and she felt herself bending beneath him, like a tree in a gorgeous, warm summer wind.

Her head fell back; her hair cascaded over his hands. He brought his lips to her throat and kissed and kissed and kissed until she felt she could support herself no longer. She murmured urgently and held on to him more tightly.

"If I were a dancer," he whispered, "I'd know just how to pick you up out of this position. But since I'm a football player—"

The next thing she knew she was tucked under his arm like an oversize football, and he was charging through the bedroom door as if on his way to the goalpost. She gasped and laughed and held on to him for dear life. "Put me down, you lug!" she cried.

He deposited her carefully on the bed, breathing deeply. "You don't weigh much," he said as he sank down beside her, "but a damn sight more than a football." He gave her a long, penetrating look, and his face turned serious. He caressed her cheek and smoothed her hair against the pillow. "Well, do I get the touchdown?"

"I think," she replied hoarsely, "you are about to 'score.'" She blushed at her brazenness, but there was something about him that swept away her inhibitions, something that allowed her to say just what she was thinking and feeling at the moment. And at this moment she was thinking how thrilling it would be to make love with him.

O'Mara blushed, too. No one had ever made him feel the way she did. He didn't have to be cool and smooth, didn't have to be the "man's man," holding up his reputation as football's finest quarterback. He could be himself, have fun with her, say whatever he needed to say to her. And he could see he brought out the spirit in her, the liveliness, the devilry she hid behind her disciplined dancer's demeanor. He liked knowing he had that effect on her. It meant more than all the touchdowns in the world, more even than the horses and pastures and white fences he was running for every time he crossed a football field.

He raised her up and took her tenderly in his arms. "You're wonderful," he whispered. "Wacky and wicked and beautiful and sexy."

Jo fastened her arms around him, leaned her head to his chest, listened to the rapid thump of his heart, felt the pounding of a different, irregular beat inside her own breast. "We've come so far, so fast," she murmured.

"Life turns around quickly sometimes. That doesn't make what we're feeling any less valid, any less sweet. We've got a long way to go together. And we can take all the time we need."

They held each other for a long time until their hearts slowed to a single rhythm. They faced the start of a journey together calmly, in tune with each other, a feeling vastly different from the preparation for it, with its excitement, its laughter, its clashes and pitfalls.

O'Mara undressed her slowly, slipping off her flat-soled boots, uncinching her belt, unbuttoning the bodice of her jersey dress. She felt the warmth of his large hands through the fabric of the dress. His touch set her body aglow. He inched the dress down to expose her shoulders, lowered the thin straps of her camisole. He kissed and caressed her neck and shoulders, exploring the well-defined bones with his hands and mouth before he slid the dress off her arms and over her slim hips.

He was amazed by the perfection of her when he peeled away her silky camisole. Her muscles were clearly defined, strong and taut, but there was also a softness about her, in her curves, in the roundness of her firm breasts, in the tangle of dark curls between her legs. "I thought I knew what your body would look like," he said quietly, "from seeing you in tights and a leotard. But I was wrong. Entirely wrong. You're gorgeous. So small, but so perfect. Looking at you makes me feel too big." He hesitated. "I'm afraid I'll hurt you."

She reached for him and began to unbutton his shirt. "You won't hurt me, O'Mara. I may be small, but I'm tough."

"There isn't a tough thing about you," he said as she dropped his shirt onto the floor. He helped her with the rest of his clothes and nestled beside her on the bed.

"Nor about you," she said as she drew her hand wonderingly over his chest. He was strong but resilient. She let her hand trail down his taut belly and over his thick thighs. Merely touching him sent an electric charge coursing through her. He stiffened slightly but noticeably each time she moved her hand, and she knew that the electricity wasn't only in her but was circulating between them.

He put his arms around her and held her close, kissed her lips lightly and raked his fingers through her hair. His hands moved from hair to neck to shoulders to back. The tip of his tongue toyed with the tip of hers. She clung to him, learned the comfort of having his body next to hers. There was so much of him . . . he covered and protected her like a large warm blanket. He was safe, secure.

When his hands and fingers had drawn the outlines of his map of her, he continued exploring with his mouth, pressing his lips to her soft neck, the hollow of her throat, the cleft between her breasts. He touched a nipple with his tongue, felt it harden and closed his lips around it carefully, lovingly. She clasped the back of his head and pressed him to her. Her excitement grew in jagged peaks as he moved his mouth to her other breast. Her breathing quickened with every minute motion of his tongue. She moaned and gasped and ran her hands up and down his back in long, hard strokes.

O'Mara felt a wanting, a needing rise in him that was greater, deeper, more insistent than any he had known. But he held himself back until he felt an equivalent desire in her. Then he entered her with agonizing slowness, letting her guide him into her hot, wet center centimeter by centimeter. He let out a long, low groan and sank into her luxurious warmth.

They pleasured each other in a leisurely way. The first jolts of excitement had subsided for both of them; they rested and readied themselves for the next waves. These were not long in arriving, for they were new to each other and their eagerness won out.

He tightened his arms around her and delved into her depths. She wrapped her strong legs around him, and they rocked each other to dizzying heights. Just when she thought she could go no higher, he brought her to a place where the air she gasped for was clear and thin, where the light was bright and blinding and came from within. He urged her onto a narrow precipice and with every stroke threatened to send her over the edge. She was so high that she was afraid of falling to unknown depths, but he pressed her on with his body, grasping her buttocks and pulling her closer. Her tension mounted, and she clung to him. With one more strong stroke she was soaring, flying free in a newly discovered stratosphere. She proclaimed her joy with a loud cry.

"Jo, Jo," he whispered huskily.

"Come with me," she bid him as she caressed his neck, his back, his buttocks.

He needed little encouragement to join her. Her words alone nearly sent him flying, but her touches and more than that, the invitation she sent him with the openness, the willingness of her body brought him to the precipice and over it. He spilled over and into her with a great heaving shudder. She held on to him as he broke through into the moment of pure, searing pleasure. And then brought him to rest in her arms.

"Astounding," he murmured when he had found his breath and voice once more.

"Mmm," she agreed as he covered her face with gentle kisses.

Seconds or minutes or hours later—they had both lost their sense of time—he settled her in the crook of his shoulder. Through the night they dozed and drifted in and out of consciousness, but they never let themselves go so far into sleep that they lost their awareness of the other.

At dawn they reached for each other once again. Their lovemaking was more refreshing than sleep, and they lay happily in each other's arms until the clock on Jo's bedside table said it was time to rouse themselves. They did so reluctantly, for they weren't eager to leave each other. But the energy and spring in their steps as they crept out of bed was not the least of the many pleasant surprises they had already shared.

7

JO EMERGED FROM THE SHOWER to find O'Mara sitting at the table busily buttering toast. The coffee she had put on while he was showering smelled incredibly delicious blended with the odor of toasting bread. He had found plates and cups in her small kitchen and taken butter, a wedge of cheese and a couple of apples out of the fridge. He jumped up when he saw her at the door and ran over to plant an exuberant kiss on her mouth. "Good morning," he practically sang. "Breakfast is ready. See how civilized and domesticated I am."

"You're a gem, O'Mara," she remarked with a happy laugh. "Do you iron and do windows, too?" She hooked her arm through his, and they walked to the table.

"I might be persuaded to, with the right incentives." He held out her chair for her and brushed aside her hair to kiss her neck as she sat down. Today, for once, she had decided to wait until the start of company class to pin up her hair. She had been amply rewarded by the warm glow the touch of his lips brought to her.

"What sort of incentives?" she asked, turning to him. A thick, damp lock of hair had fallen onto his forehead, and she pushed it back with a finger, ran the same finger down his cheek and along the line of his jaw.

"A kiss or two." He cupped her face with his hands and applied his lips tenderly to hers once and then again. "Or three." He took another lingering nibble at her lips. "Ah, Jo," he said with a sigh, and crouched beside her. "I feel like I could do anything today, as if I *would* do anything today, as long as I knew I'd have another night with you that was even half as terrific as last night."

She was touched, delighted, even a little bit humbled by his ardent speech. "You don't have to conquer the world to make it happen again," she said gently.

He put his arms around her waist. "What do I have to do?"

"Nothing. Just be yourself."

"Do you mean that?"

"Of course I do," she chided.

He pulled himself away from her and took his place at the table. "Do you know how much freedom that gives me?" She looked at him questioningly. "It only occurred to me last night. I don't have to be a star quarterback with you, I don't have to call the shots, be the big man." He picked up an apple to quarter and core. "I've been looking for a woman who could do that for me for a long time." He grinned and shook his head. "It just took me a while to recognize the package."

Jo got up to retrieve the coffee from the kitchen and rested her hand on his shoulder as she tipped the pot over his cup. "You were the last thing I expected to walk into my life, too. But here I am pouring your coffee." She returned his grin and shake of the head.

They finished eating, and O'Mara started to pour her another cup of coffee, but she put her hand over her cup. "As much as I'd love to spend the rest of the day with you, I've really got to run." She pushed back her chair and dashed into the bedroom to find some clean tights and a leotard. Her Sunday laundry routine had been interrupted yesterday, and she had to root around in her bureau before coming across some old spares. A look at the hastily made bed as she left the room made her wonder how she could carry on normally for the rest of the day, the rest of the week.

While she was gone O'Mara cleared the table and shrugged into his sport jacket. He wasn't eager to leave her; he, too, would have loved for them to spend the day together. But he felt fresh, ready to tackle the problems of pulling the Empire together with renewed vigor, so that the thought of going to practice wasn't unpleasant. He doubted anything could be unpleasant this morning. He felt so good and so hopeful that the impossible challenge the team posed seemed as easy as breaking a straw in two. "Shall I drop you off?" he asked when she came out of the bedroom.

"No, thanks. I need the walk." She needed some time to make the transition between him and the rest of her life. He was not going to fit neatly into her tightly organized world, but fit he would. She would see to that. They both would.

"I understand. I need the drive to the stadium." He held out his arms, and she walked into them. He held her tight.

"I never thanked you properly for the ticket," she said softly.

He was concentrating on the luscious smell of her hair, inhaling it, memorizing it. "What ticket?" he murmured.

"To the game, of course. The one you sent with the enormous box of chocolates."

He pulled away from her and took her by the shoulders. "What are you talking about?"

"The ticket and chocolate truffles you had delivered here last Monday. You can't have forgotten." She looked at him closely to see if he was kidding, but his face showed no sign of levity. On the contrary, his eyes had narrowed, his mouth was set. Tension had begun to show in his neck.

"I didn't send you any ticket," he said suspiciously. "Or any truffles."

"If you didn't, who did?" she asked reasonably.

"You tell me." He scowled at her and crossed his arms over his chest. He didn't like the sound of this. Not one bit.

"How should I know? I assumed it was from you."

"Why would you assume that?"

"Because who else would send me a ticket to an Empire game and a box of truffles?" Why was he giving her that accusatory look, she asked herself. What was going on here?

O'Mara was starting to simmer. Someone was playing games with him again, and it was making him furious. "You mean to tell me you used a ticket when you didn't know who gave it to you?"

"I told you. I thought you'd sent it."

"I didn't," he said flatly.

"You didn't?"

"*No!*"

"What are you getting so upset about?" She took a step away from him. An astounding, unsettling change was taking place in him right before her eyes.

He slammed a fist into the palm of his other hand. "He's doing it again. That lousy owner. Trying to drive me crazy. He's throwing us together for some reason. First that dinner in his box, now this ticket. The owner sent a pass to the players' lounge, too, didn't he? I was surprised to see you there yesterday, but I figured you'd asked somebody at the ballet to get you one. It was all a setup, wasn't it?"

"A setup for what? I don't understand."

He began to pace between the dining alcove and the bedroom door. "He must want to spy on me, but how he thinks that's going to help I don't know." He turned to Jo. "He picked a good accomplice, though. When your legs give out you can apply to the CIA. I'm sure they'd be thrilled to have you."

Something had gone desperately wrong. "Look here, Fred—" she used the nickname to emphasize her anger "—I don't know what you're talking about. I've told you before, and I'll tell you again. I thought you sent me the ticket."

"Tell it to the marines, Jo." He wrenched open the door and stalked out into the hall. "And don't call me Fred!" he yelled back caustically and stomped on.

Jo was so stunned she couldn't move. Only at the sound of the front door's slamming did her brain clear and issue commands to her legs. She raced into the hall and through the vestibule, but by the time she'd run down to the stoop, O'Mara was already in the Jag. He gunned the motor and peeled out of the parking spot.

I'll be late for class, was all she could think of. She rushed inside for her bag, locked the door and flew down the street. She reached her place at the *barre* just as the pianist was about to begin the first exercise. For a blessed hour and a half she didn't have to think about what had happened.

Getting through the rehearsal that followed was another story. Her body could perform the class exercises on automatic pilot, the combinations that followed with a minimum of concentration. But a rehearsal demanded full alertness. Even though the session was a review of a ballet she had danced countless times, she stumbled over the steps, lost her place in the music, made premature entrances. Her colleagues joked about it at first, wondering if she was still asleep or had put her toe shoes on the wrong feet. But by the end of the two hours they were grousing and griping at her. Sasha told her quite sharply as they left the studio to get herself together before the rehearsal for his new ballet that afternoon.

Jo walked glumly to her locker after the rehearsal, trying to work out the puzzle. How, in the space of five minutes, could O'Mara have tossed aside all that had happened between them the night before? How could he believe she had a part in any duplicity against him? She simply couldn't understand it. And couldn't he see that she had been manipulated just as much as he? That was almost as maddening as having him pin the blame on her. They'd both been duped, but all he could think of was himself. She climbed into a warm-up suit and slammed her locker shut with a bang. It didn't make her feel any better.

She left the locker room and started toward the cafeteria, wondering if food would stem the unpleasant gnawing in the pit of her stomach, when Mrs. Charles's secretary approached her. The summons to the director's office came as no surprise. Suzanne Charles may not have set foot in the rehearsal studio that morning, but she had no doubt heard of Jo's poor performance.

Sometimes Jo thought the woman could see through walls.

Mrs. Charles looked over the top of her half-moon-shaped reading glasses when Jo walked into her office. "Sit down, Jo, I'll be with you in a moment," she said briskly.

Jo took a seat on the sofa. Outside the window the Hudson flowed on, sparkling in the sun. She eyed it resentfully. She felt so changed, so torn apart. How could the river look the same as it had yesterday, last week, last month, last year? Unreasonably, she expected the world to somehow reflect her inner turmoil. But Mrs. Charles's office was as tidy as ever, Mrs. Charles herself as impeccably groomed and composed.

There was a knock at the door. "Would you get that, please? I've asked for lunch to be sent down." *Oh, dear*, Jo thought as she walked to the door, *this isn't going to be just a pep talk, this is serious.*

The tray she took from the cafeteria worker held two tuna salad sandwiches on whole wheat bread, two glasses of skim milk and two bowls of fruit salad.

"Put it on the coffee table, dear." Mrs. Charles took off her reading glasses, folded them and put them in their case. She joined Jo on the sofa.

Jo decided to take the bull by the horns. "I'm sorry I was such a mess at rehearsal this morning. It was just one of those mornings. I'm sure I'll be fine this afternoon."

"I'm sure you will, too." Mrs. Charles took a napkin from the tray and placed it over her lap. "Everyone has an off-day now and then. Especially after they've had a late night."

Jo practically had to hold her jaw with her hand to keep it from dropping. Not only could the woman see through walls, she was positively psychic. "Er, I was out last night. But not that late," she hedged.

Mrs. Charles reached for the copy of the morning's *Daily News* and pointed to a red-circled paragraph in a gossip column. Jo was shocked to read her own name. And O'Mara's. They'd been seen at Neptune. She kept her eyes glued to the paper, waiting for Mrs. Charles to express her disappointment. But the words that reached Jo were as unexpected as seeing her name in the paper had been.

"It's about time you were out and about more, Jo," Mrs. Charles told her.

"It is?"

"Of course. All work and no play..."

"Makes Jo a dull girl," she muttered. *I'd rather be dull than have the dull ache I have in my chest now.*

"Not dull, my dear. Less satisfied. And in the long run less capable." Mrs. Charles picked up her sandwich and urged Jo to eat, as well.

Jo took a small bite and somehow managed to swallow it.

"Do you know when my career really blossomed, Jo, dear? After I met Oliver. He didn't know the first thing about ballet, but what he taught me about love and life changed me. I was a competent soloist; I became..." She paused modestly.

"A legend," Jo supplied. Suzanne London was the first prima ballerina the newly formed Metropolitan Ballet had produced. She brought the company a fiercely loyal following. She danced until she was in her mid-forties and then took over the administration of the company. For ten years she had used Oliver Charles's influential banking and business connections to build as firm a financial base for the company as any American artistic organization in existence.

Suzanne Charles dismissed Jo's praise with a small wave of her hand, not because it wasn't deserved but because it was unimportant to her now. "What you must do, Jo, is to keep your work fresh, dance not only with skill, with understanding, with passion—but with joy, as well. You're very close to the top, my dear. Don't shy away."

"I'll try not to," Jo answered stiffly. She was close to tears. She knew what Mrs. Charles meant when she talked about joy and freshness; she'd had her first lesson last night. But how could she remember that, use it in her work after O'Mara had walked out on her? She was in an impossible situation.

"Finish your milk, Jo." Mrs. Charles was businesslike once more. "And tell me how the classes with the football players are going."

Oh, no, Jo cried inwardly, *I'll have to see him tomorrow, teach him in the class.* "Okay, I guess. The team seems to be winning." She smiled wanly.

"Oliver would have loved the game they played yesterday," Mrs. Charles said with relish. "Did you see it?"

"Yes," she answered without elaborating.

"Oliver may have remained as ignorant about ballet as he was when he met me, but I picked up a point or two about football over the years." Mrs. Charles made a few suggestions for Jo's classes based on what she'd seen on the field the day before. Then she picked up the newspaper and handed it to Jo. "You'd better run along. Take this with you, and make sure Sasha sees it. I doubt he'll like it, but it will do him good to see that his partner has stepped into the spotlight, too."

Jo took the paper, thanked Mrs. Charles for the lunch and started for the door. She stopped and turned back. "I'll remember what you said." She didn't want Mrs. Charles to think her ungrateful. The director didn't often speak openly or intimately to members of the company, and Jo knew how special it was to have been singled out as she had been. The talk had convinced her of Mrs. Charles's confidence in her, but it had also come at a time when the advice was very painful for her to hear.

"I'm sure you will, dear," Mrs. Charles said kindly. "And one last thing, Jo. Patti Pringle and a video crew will be at the class tomorrow. This is just the sort of publicity we'd hoped to get from the arrangement with the Empire."

The admonition in Mrs. Charles's voice was clear. "I understand. I'll be on my best behavior," she promised.

"I'm sure you will."

Jo closed the door behind her and leaned against it for a moment. It was only midday, but she already felt like an action-packed week had passed since that morning. She pointed her feet resolutely in the direction of the rehearsal studio. *Freshness and joy, freshness and joy,* she repeated to herself as she walked down the hall.

8

PATTI PRINGLE WAS the closest thing to an Amazon that Jo had ever encountered or expected to encounter. Although she'd seen the reporter on her television show, the woman had always been seated. Standing in her low-heeled pumps, Patti Pringle was six feet tall and stunningly feminine, with sandy-brown hair that fell in soft waves to her shoulders, a face that belonged on a classical sculpture and a statuesque body. She looked every inch the gold-medal Olympic track-and-field athlete that she had been before setting her sights on a new goal—becoming the country's foremost female sports journalist. Even Jo knew she had changed men's attitudes about women's understanding of sports. She had entrée to as many locker rooms and strategy rooms as there were major league teams, in any sport.

"I'm pleased to meet you," Jo said, very much aware of how small and delicate her hand felt in Pringle's strong grip.

"And you. Teaching this class is quite a departure for you," Pringle stated as she took a small notebook and pen from her shoulder bag.

She outlined the highlights of Jo's career as she would have quoted the professional statistics of an athlete. She's certainly done her homework, Jo thought, and doubtless seen the gossip column item. It was going to be hard enough to see O'Mara, but the thought of doing so under Patti Pringle's keen powers of observation made the task seem positively Herculean. Jo reined her emotions and replied to the reporter's opening statement. "It is a challenge," she agreed.

"Why do you think you were picked?"

"Probably because I didn't know one end of a football field from another," she answered, and forced out what she hoped was a gay-sounding laugh.

Pringle smiled but wasn't about to be diverted from her task by a mere attempt at levity. "And do you now?"

"I'm learning."

"What's the team learning from you?"

The reporter's rapid-fire questions didn't give her much time to think, but she supposed that was deliberate. A journalist like Patti Pringle wouldn't want pat answers. Jo wanted to give the best impression possible of the company while avoiding any questions about her relationship with O'Mara. "Grace, agility, the discipline of coordinating mind and body," she replied, hoping her answer was satisfactory.

"How are they doing?"

"Very well, now that they've gotten over the initial culture shock." Pringle reacted with a knowing nod, and Jo started to feel she was holding her own in the interview.

"Who are your star pupils?"

Oh, no, here it comes, Jo thought with a sinking feeling. But her answer was straightforward, with no inflection in her voice. "O'Mara and Washington."

Pringle flipped her notebook closed. "It looks like I'm going to get a chance to find out for myself."

The men were beginning to filter into the room. They had abandoned their elephant T-shirts for the regulation plain white ones, and they seemed to swagger all the more to compensate for the shirts' absence and Patti Pringle's presence. Pringle greeted the men by name as they passed her. Few of them looked her in the eye, just muttered and strutted past, trying to pretend there was nothing out of the ordinary about being seen in tights and ballet slippers. The same men who had been so friendly to Jo in the players' lounge after Sunday's game gave her closemouthed nods or at best reluctant hellos.

O'Mara, however, greeted the reporter effusively. "How ya doin', Pringle?" He gave her a hearty handshake and clapped her on the back with exaggerated camaraderie.

"Fine, O'Mara. Yourself?" Pringle stood her ground, didn't give in to his too-friendly greeting.

O'Mara mugged a grin and a wink and gave her a thumbs-up signal. He gave Jo a breezy good-morning, as if he had no more relationship with her than with a supermarket checker. She watched him out of the corner of her eye for any signs of pleasure or displeasure with her, but his facade didn't alter as he took his place at the front of the *barre* for the start of class.

Pringle signaled to the video crew who had accompanied her, and they conferred briefly with Jo. The pianist took his place, and she began the first set of *pliés*.

During the *barre* work she tried her best to ignore O'Mara and concentrate on the rest of her students, but her mind, her eyes kept straying back to him. The mere sight of him, the knowledge of exactly what lay beneath the thin covering of tights and T-shirt excited her, brought back the indescribable beauty of their night together. Perhaps his studious nonchalance meant that the same images were romping in his head, she thought hopefully. But a more realistic inner voice told her it probably meant he was concentrating on controlling his temper in front of the press.

When she brought the class to the center of the floor, O'Mara positioned himself directly in front of her, hands clasped in front of him like an eager and obedient student. He looked at her in a way that said, "See how good I'm being." Immediately she had an irresistible impulse to goad him into losing his maddening cool. She knew she couldn't do anything that would jeopardize the press coverage, but she could egg him on a little, see just how calm and collected he could keep himself.

"In the last couple of weeks," she addressed the class, "we've worked on leaps and turns. That was the fun part," she said with a grin, and elicited a groan from the class. They had settled down some after realizing that Patti Pringle and her crew hadn't gone into hysterics after watching them perform the opening exercises. "Now we're going to work on something difficult. Balance. You all want to be well balanced, don't you?" she asked brightly, sending O'Mara a sugary smile.

"Hey, Jo," someone called from the back of the room, "you dance better than you tell jokes."

Everyone laughed except O'Mara, who turned and growled, "Cut the comedy, wise guys."

"It's okay, Twink, I can take it." She enjoyed O'Mara's flash of annoyance at the nickname the men had given him. She wondered if she'd be pushing it if she called him Fred. A glance at Patti Pringle flipping a new page in her notebook answered her question.

"Yeah, cool it, Twinkle Toes," Rory put in. "We can take some bad jokes if it makes us dance good. And keep winning."

O'Mara shot an evil look at Rory but quickly composed himself and returned his eyes to the front, refolding his hands. Jo began to see the effort he was making, which meant she was making progress.

She clapped her hands for attention and began to explain the new movement. "This is called *dévelopé*, gentlemen." She demonstrated by pointing her bent knee to the side and drawing her foot slowly up the inside of her left leg until her right foot was touching the inside of her left knee. The position made her resemble a stork standing on one leg. She continued to demonstrate as she spoke. "We will now extend the leg from this position, once to the front, *en face*, once to the side, *à la seconde*, and once to the back, *en arrière*." She narrowed her eyes and warned, "Don't even think of snickering, you guys—it's *arrière*, not *derrière*."

This drew a laugh, and Jo felt her first flicker of enjoyment since Monday morning. Normality might return to her life, after all, she thought as she dropped her leg and continued her explanation. "The point of the exercise is not to get your leg as high as you can, not immediately, but to learn to stand on one leg while moving the other in a careful, controlled, long manner. The movement must take place in the leg only, no swiveling of hips allowed. Would you mind demonstrating, Fred? Er, I mean Mr. O'Mara?"

He glared at her hotly but answered with excessive cordiality. "Of course not."

She asked him to face the class, then stood behind him and put her hands on his hips. She felt him flinch slightly at her touch, felt her own hands and face grow warm. She had a second's doubt that she could continue to sabotage O'Mara into losing his temper without giving herself away. But she brought forth a cool, professional demeanor. "Please begin to lift your right leg, toes pointed, knee turned out. Slowly," she cautioned when he jerked his foot off the floor. "Raise it only as high as you can without moving your hip. Good, good," she coached. She talked him through the exercise, helping him keep his balance as he performed the difficult movement. The longer she kept her hands on his hips the more she wondered if she were sabotaging herself more than O'Mara.

Finally he completed the movements. They were careful not to look at each other as they separated, and Jo quickly called for music and left O'Mara to circulate among the men as they teetered and tottered and gritted their teeth. *Dévelopés* required a combination of control and balance that most of the men found impossible to maintain. Even O'Mara and Washington were having a hard time with the movement. But she saw today in the team—despite the presence of Patti Pringle and the crew, despite the silent tug-of-war between her and O'Mara—a gritty determination to succeed.

After teaching the *dévelopé*, Jo reviewed the leaps and turns they had learned in the previous classes, and by then the class time was nearly spent. She led the team in the final bow and dismissed them.

Pringle came to Jo immediately and thanked her. "This is going to be one of the best stories of my career. I really enjoyed myself." She asked Jo a few questions on technical points and then excused herself to talk to the players.

With the team huddled around Pringle there was no reason for Jo to stay, but she remained in the front of the room for a moment or so. O'Mara was standing behind the cluster of his teammates, and she tried to catch his eye. A strong current still flowed between them. She felt it even with O'Mara across the room. There was no reason they couldn't talk over their misunderstanding. No reason except his foul temper. But he refused to look in her direction.

She began to feel foolish, standing all by herself. She made a final attempt to get his attention, but he ignored her. *All right*, she thought gloomily, *if that's the way he wants to play it*. She marched out of the classroom without looking back.

O'MARA KNEW JO WAS TRYING to catch his eye, but he was damned if he'd give her the satisfaction of looking her way. What he couldn't understand and couldn't forgive himself for was the way he'd started to feel when she'd put her hands on his hips during class. He was still fuming mad at her for playing the innocent, for pretending she wasn't in cahoots with the lousy Emperor, but he was having a helluva time taming his body. And with these flimsy tights he'd have been a locker-room joke for the rest of his life if he hadn't managed to control his all-too-natural reaction to her touch.

He fixed his attention on a spot on the ceiling and waited impatiently until he was left alone with Pringle. "Okay," he said when the last player had gone out the door, "I got you your exclusive story. When do you make good on your part of the deal?"

"When I find the answer, O'Mara," she said dryly. "We only made the deal yesterday, and believe it or not I have other things to do besides find out who owns the Empire. I don't see why you're making a major issue out of this. What difference does it make?"

"I like to pull my own strings, Pringle. You of all people should understand that."

"Sure, but don't you think you're beating your head against a brick wall? Since the story of the sale broke, every lead I've had has dead-ended. Me and six hundred other reporters," she said with a wry look. "I did, however, come up with one very interesting tidbit."

"What is it?"

"I know someone who covers the sports industry for an investment banking firm. He owed me a favor, so I asked him to poke around, see who owns stock in the Empire."

"Everybody knows there's no one with a controlling interest, at least on record. It's got to be hidden somewhere."

"I know that," Pringle said impatiently. "Did you ever stop to think about this ballet setup, O'Mara? There must be a hundred ballet schools in this city. Why did the owner pick the Metropolitan Ballet?"

"You tell me," he said, very interested in her line of reasoning.

"The Metropolitan Ballet owns about five percent of the stock through its employee pension fund. There might be a connection. I'm going to run it down."

"You do that," he said evenly. Inside he was seething. Pringle's evidence meant that the owner *was* connected somehow with the ballet. That made Jo all the more guilty in his eyes. And she'd had the nerve to pull

that butter-wouldn't-melt-in-my-mouth act with him
that morning. Twink, indeed. She was one hundred and
five pounds of pure nerve.

"Yo, O'Mara, you still with me?"

O'Mara shook himself out of his thoughts. "Yeah,
yeah, I'm with you."

Pringle started toward the door and motioned to
O'Mara to come with her. "What's going on between
you and the ballerina?" she asked.

"Nothing," he said flatly.

"Come on, I read the whole paper, not just the sports
pages. This is strictly off the record," she cajoled.
"Friend to friend."

"We had a couple of dates. It didn't work out."

"Ha!" she scoffed. "There's something going on. I can
smell it. She's nice, O'Mara. She's got class, style. She
seems like she'd be a good match for you."

And she's a rotten traitor. "No further comment," he
said firmly to Pringle. "On or off the record."

She held up her hand. "I get the message. I have to
be going. Thanks for putting in a good word for me. I've
got a great feeling about this story. It's going to be one
of my best ever." She clapped her arm around his
shoulder, and they went out into the hall together.

"You'll call me as soon as you know anything more?"
he asked.

"Right. But don't expect miracles." They walked to
the locker-room door together. "Well, thanks again.
This has been a truly enlightening morning for me."

She dangled the statement before him like bait before a fish, daring him to bite. "Oh, yeah?" he growled
suspiciously.

"Yeah." A slow smile spread over her face. "I never knew what cute buns you had before."

"How would you like me to make your dentist a very happy man, Pringle?"

"Woman, O'Mara. My dentist is a woman."

"You always have to have the last word, don't you?" he asked with a tolerant grin. You could always be sure to get as good as you gave with Pringle. When they made her they broke the mold. And what a mold it had been. Buddies or no, he appreciated a beautiful woman, no matter how smart a mouth she had.

"That's what they pay me for." She patted him on the cheek and started off down the hall.

"Take care, Patti," he said, and walked into the locker room. Now why couldn't he have fallen for someone sensible like Pringle, someone who knew a touchdown from a punt? No, he had to fall head over heels for some shrimp of a ballerina. He could deny it from now till next July, but there it was. Plain as the nose on his face. He slammed his foot hard against his locker door, forgetting he was wearing ballet slippers instead of his usual spikes. How could she have done it, he railed as he nursed his throbbing toe.

While O'Mara changed he started thinking about ways in which the ballet company and the team could be linked. Maybe Jo's story about growing up in an ordinary New York City suburb was as phony as she was. Maybe she had a rich daddy. Or sugar daddy. Which made what she had done to him even worse. Or maybe the answer was something outlandish, something to do with that Trevetsky. Maybe he was some sort of double agent. *Now you're getting crazy, O'Mara. What use*

*would the Russians have for a football team? But then
you never know.*

All afternoon he kept moving around the meager
parts of his puzzle, but he couldn't come up with anything that made sense, even as a thin and unlikely plot
for a television show. But he couldn't shut his brain off.
Even after his third stupid mistake of the afternoon, he
couldn't stop thinking about it. And her. Jo was always there, dancing around in his head. She was like a
movie he couldn't walk out of: he was strapped to the
seat with his eyes permanently open.

The first thing he did when he got home from practice was to phone Pringle. "What have you got?" he
asked without preliminaries when she picked up the
phone.

"Cul-de-sac city, O'Mara. Another dead end. Suzanne Charles told me the Empire stock was a gift to the
pension fund from her late husband. Apparently he was
a fan. The value of the stock skyrocketed with all the
publicity, so of course she and the ballet's trustees are
holding on to it. She said she was approached by the
owner's mouthpiece, what's his name, Chapin, to ar-
range for the teaching. That's all she knows."

"And you believe her?"

"I've got a pretty good nose. She sounds on the level
to me. I'll see what I can find out about her personal finances. If her husband was a fan, she might have an interest herself. But I doubt it. My hunch is her story will
check out."

"Okay," he said dispiritedly.

"Hey, perk up there, buddy. I'll figure this out yet. But
it's going to take some time. This isn't the kind of information I can get from the public library, you know."

"Yeah, I know." He hung up and plopped himself down on the couch. He could use a drink, but he didn't feel like getting up to fix one. He could use a meal, too, but putting one together was too much of a bother. He stared at the blank wall opposite the sofa for a long time. He kept meaning to spruce up the apartment, but he never got around to it. The place was just for sleeping and eating, not for living. Everything he cared about was up at the farm.

The thought had barely taken root before he was out the door. He grabbed his jacket and raced for the elevator. In the Jag he could be there in under two hours. He could get up at dawn and see the horses before he'd have to leave to get to practice on time. Even with all the driving, a night there would be a damned sight better than sitting here staring at these blank walls all night.

Because there was only one thing that mattered more to him than the farm....

9

OCTOBER SLIPPED AWAY quietly. The days got colder and shorter, and Jo got busier and busier. Only two weeks remained before the ballet's season opened. The rehearsal schedule was taking on its usual frantic preopening pace, with choreographers, costumers, conductors and technical crews competing for time and space. There was never enough of either to go around at this time of year. Plus she had the added responsibility of teaching the team.

Surprisingly, she didn't find the teaching a burden. On the contrary, her few hours a week with the Empire began to seem like a haven of sanity in the madhouse the Metropolitan became before the season's opening night. The time she spent preparing her classes gave her a needed break from her concerns about the roles, especially the new one that she would be dancing. She found a great release from the preseason tension and her O'Mara-inspired worries in listening to and choosing music for the class, in thinking of new ways to combine steps or to explain them.

The team was still winning, not every game but enough to have moved them from the bottom to the middle of the standings in their division. That was certainly a boost to their morale, but she saw more subtle changes taking place in the men. They would never be dancers, but they were developing a real respect for what she was teaching them. She saw them using it, too, on the field, in the few snatches of the games she was able to catch. Not that they were all leaping and pirouetting the way O'Mara had done in the first two games she'd seen him play. But they had better balance, more agility. They were thinking faster on their feet, getting into less jams and getting out of them more easily. She couldn't believe that the improvements since she'd begun teaching the team were entirely coincidental, and she took a great deal of satisfaction from her achievement. That helped balance the anxieties she was feeling on other scores.

Sasha was demanding superhuman perfection from the dancers in his ballet. He had no tolerance for even the slightest mistake. She had the crucial role, so she came in for most of his sharp, crushing criticism. She had tried to explain that he was making her more nervous and mistake prone, but her attempt had only made him more unreasonable and demanding.

And then there was O'Mara. He was perfectly civil to her, icy cold but entirely polite when they had to speak. But several times she had caught him looking at her as if she were some strange mutant or an alien from another planet. And once, just once, but how she had cherished the moment, she had seen him looking at her with the most intense, poignant longing. That day she had tried to approach him after class, but he'd brushed her off, pushed her to one side like unwanted food on a plate. She didn't know how much more she could take. Every time she thought about it, she couldn't imagine going into that classroom again, but she couldn't let Mrs. Charles and now the team down. She also couldn't let herself down. Jo Sherbourne was not a quitter.

The Thursday before the opening, she walked to the classroom feeling as if all her joints had been glued together. The rehearsal for Sasha's ballet had lasted until after two that morning. She was stretched to the limit of her physical and mental capacities. And she could hardly face the thought of O'Mara's black looks when all she wanted was for him to take her in his arms, comfort her, tell her she'd not only get through this opening but score a great success in it. The thought of having to deal with him nearly defeated her.

She heard an unusual amount of talking when she opened the door, and it took a moment for her to realize it wasn't chatter but grumbling. The men were gathered around O'Mara, obviously unhappy about something. "What's going on?" she asked.

"We've just been issued a royal summons to your opening night," O'Mara answered sharply, waving a piece of paper and an envelope at her as if it were a red cape and she were the bull.

"You ought to be pleased," Jo told him as coolly as she could. "I hear it's one of the hottest tickets in town."

"You want to talk hot," he shouted at her, "take a look at the tempers in this room!"

"Not the least of which is yours," she retorted testily.

"The unmitigated gall of that so and so," O'Mara continued, as if he hadn't heard her. "Just listen to this." He read from the paper he'd waved at her.

"All team members will report to the opening performance of the Metropolitan Ballet on Monday, November 19th, 8:00 p.m., Metropolitan Hall.

Tickets, contained herein, will be the responsibility of Mr. O'Mara and will be distributed by him on the evening of the performance. A second ticket, for the guest of his choice, has been provided for each player. Attendance is mandatory. Failure to appear will result in fines and suspension. Only serious illness will allow a player to be excused.

"I can't stand it," he ranted. "How does this guy think we can play for him if he treats us like this?"

Rory Washington stepped up to O'Mara and put a hand on his shoulder. "Cool it, man," he said quietly. "This isn't Jo's fault. She didn't write the letter or send the tickets."

"Of course," O'Mara said sarcastically, his words aimed in her direction like poisoned darts. "She didn't know anything about it."

"I only dance with the ballet, I don't sell—or give away—the tickets," she told him wearily. Why did everything the blasted owner did get blamed on her? She didn't have the faintest idea who he was, nor did she care. O'Mara had to have a short circuit in his brain if he thought she did.

"These clowns are all het up," Rory said to her kindly, "because it means they have to miss watching the game of the week on TV. Tell you what, fellas, why doesn't somebody videotape it, then nobody has to miss anything."

Jo smiled her thanks at Rory. He had manners and decency no matter what happened, unlike his quarterback.

"That's not the whole story, Washington," another player called out.

Rory turned to her again. "Some of the guys feel that, well, they don't mind so much taking the lessons anymore, but they don't see how being forced to watch the company dance is going to help our game."

"I'm sure I don't know what your owner had in mind," she said pointedly, her gaze leveled at O'Mara, "but it seems to me that seeing a ballet performed might help you see how much you've learned. Besides that, I think you'll enjoy it, even if you don't understand it all or you wish you were home watching the game."

"Will you be dancing?" someone asked grudgingly.

"Yes. I'll be dancing the principal role in Alexander Trevetsky's new ballet. You'll be among the first people in the world to see it. And Alex and I will be doing the principal roles in *Birdland*. You saw a segment of that ballet during the second class." She explained the rest of the program and answered a couple of questions. "We should get started now. There's a lot to be covered today, and we've already used up the first ten minutes of class. Will you please take your places at the *barre*?"

The door opened just as she finished speaking, and Mrs. Charles entered the room. "Good morning, gentlemen, Jo. I'm sorry to interrupt, but I've just had a call from Mr. Chapin to say that you will be attending Monday night's performance. I'm delighted you'll be in the audience, and I'm delighted with the excitement the collaboration between the Empire and the Metropolitan has generated." Since Patti Pringle's nationally syndicated show had aired, the Metropolitan had received a flurry of publicity. "I must say this is just the result I had hoped for when I entered into the agreement. I must say I was rather wary at first. I'm not used to dealing with go-betweens. But everything seems to have worked out so very well for everyone."

Mrs. Charles beamed at the players, and they shuffled uncomfortably in their places. O'Mara wasn't the only one who didn't like being reminded that their professional lives were being run by someone they didn't know. "We always have a wonderful party after the performance, and I hope you will all join us, with your wives or dates, of course, whom I understand have also been provided with tickets. Have a good class, gentlemen, and a good game on Sunday. We'll be rooting for you. And we hope you'll be rooting for us on Monday. As it's bound to be a late night for all concerned, why don't we cancel the following morning's class. I'm sure I can get authorization through Mr. Chapin." She apologized again to Jo for the intrusion and left the studio.

Mrs. Charles's suggestion seemed to go down well with the team. They didn't seem quite as resentful when Jo clapped her hands and asked them once again to go to the *barre*. It was awfully nice of Mrs. Charles to invite the team to the party. Most of the other people on the guest list had donated thousands of dollars to the company. She wondered if any of them would be happier about attending if they knew how much money they had just saved.

"Hey, Jo, will there be champagne and caviar at this shindig?" one of the bulkiest tackles asked.

"There usually is," she told him.

"But they serve it by the spoonful, not the pound, Nowicki," one of his buddies gibed.

"Okay, that's enough," Jo cautioned. "I'd like every-one to close his eyes, take a deep breath, focus on the class and exhale. Once more, please." When the men had settled down she began the class, but she found she had a difficult time forgetting O'Mara's behavior toward her.

I've really had enough of him treating me like a lep-er, she thought as she watched the men leaping across the floor in pairs during the final minutes of the class. She stopped thinking about O'Mara long enough to notice and be pleased that all of them had mastered the step and that most of them were even moving in time with the music. But her pleasure was fleeting. The way he had acted this morning riled her more than all his scowls and barbed comments put together. She had to get him to talk to her, talk with her. The burden was too heavy to carry around in these last hectic days before the opening. She couldn't handle any extra baggage weighing her down.

As the men were leaving, she said loud enough for everyone to hear, "Can I talk to you, O'Mara?"

"I'm busy," he said curtly, and headed toward the door.

"It's important," she insisted and planted herself in front of him.

Once again Rory came to her aid. He put a restrain-ing hand on O'Mara's arm. "Give the lady a break, man. She only wants to talk to you, although why she wants to give a rude son of a gun like you the time of day beats—"

"I hear you," O'Mara interrupted. "I hear you."

Rory winked at Jo. "Don't be too hard on him. He's been touchy with everyone lately. All you have to do is look at him the wrong way, and you almost get your head bit off."

"I'll be gentle," Jo said ironically.

"Don't you worry any about the team on Monday, Jo. Once they see you up there on the stage they'll come around. And you've already got one fan. I'll be the one shoutin' and whistlin'."

"Thanks, Rory. I hope you catch some good ones on Sunday—if you get thrown any, that is."

"I thought you said you were going to be gentle," he replied with a soft whistle.

"If you two are through with the cheerful banter," O'Mara said caustically, "do you think we could get this tête-à-tête under way?"

Rory squeezed Jo's hand and hurried out the door.

O'Mara took a belligerent stance, feet planted wide, arms crossed over his chest. "Well?" he demanded.

"Oh, cut it out." He was too exasperating, putting on a show of defiance when all she wanted was a civil discussion. "Can't you stand there like a normal person and hear me out?"

He forced himself to relax his posture. There was no sense acting like a teenager called onto the carpet. "What do you want to tell me?" he said with all the reasonableness he could muster.

"I don't want to tell you anything, O'Mara. I want to have a conversation with you, I—"

"We don't have anything to say," he interrupted.

"Yes, we do." She was determined to stay calm and speak in a reasonable tone. "You seem to have gotten it into your head that I not only know who the owner is but that I also tell him what to do. I told you that morning when you walked out on me that I don't. I don't know why you won't believe me." She felt a sob burning the back of her throat and swallowed hard to chase it away.

"Because your story seems unbelievable, especially in light of the financial connections that exist between the Metropolitan and the Empire."

"What financial connections?" she asked, bewildered.

"That's just what I mean, Jo." He grabbed her shoulders and held her firmly. "If you'd only come clean with me," he said passionately, desperately. It was killing him to be so close to her, touching her yet not able to take her into his arms.

"But I have." She lowered her eyes, afraid they would reveal too much of what she was feeling, the longing more than the hurt. "Don't you think I'd tell you if I knew? Do you know me so little to think that I could have been the way I was with you that night because someone told me to do it?"

A sharp pain pierced O'Mara's chest. He let go of her, dropping his hands heavily to his sides. No, he couldn't think that of her, not when she asked him that way, her voice raw, her body trembling. He didn't know what to think. He had been so sure that morning, had been even more convinced when Pringle uncovered the Empire stock in the Metropolitan's pension portfolio. But Pringle had come up with now new connections along that line in two weeks of digging. He'd have to think this whole thing through again.

"Can you answer me?" she asked in a small voice. "At least tell me that you heard what I said?"

"I heard you, Jo. I don't know what to say. Honestly, I don't." He turned quickly and left the room.

Jo closed up the classroom and walked slowly to the locker room, thinking about what had just happened. Her thoughts were all gloomy at first, but as she climbed into her warm-up suit a glimmer of hope broke through her sadness. No, he may not have answered her, but she had gotten through to him this time. He had listened. He had heard her. As she left the room she felt as though a weight had been lifted from her shoulders, and if she didn't bounce upstairs to get her lunch, her steps were lighter and more resilient than they had been in weeks.

O'MARA TOSSED HIS CARTONS of Chinese takeout onto the kitchen counter and pulled a beer from the fridge. He settled himself on the sofa and put on the evening news. But the events of the world were far from his mind; it was the events of the morning he focused on. When the phone rang he answered it with a distracted "Yeah?" He perked up when he heard Pringle's voice on the line.

"I did it," she said triumphantly. "I know who it is. I need to figure out a couple more things and get a few more facts, but with any luck I'll be able to report it on next week's show."

"Don't keep me in suspense, Pringle. Who is it?"

"You're gonna love this. It's the man we all love to hate, Barton Harley."

O'Mara could have been knocked down with a feather. Harley was the autocratic owner of the Texas baseball club that had won the World Series just weeks before. Harley fired managers at the drop of a hat, cowed his players into winning performances. He was

just the sort of man who would have pulled the stunts
that had made O'Mara so furious.

"Are you still there?" Pringle asked. O'Mara grunted,
and she continued with her news. "He's got a lot of
stock in the Empire but hidden in a lot of dummy cor-
porations. What I've found out about so far doesn't
seem to be the controlling interest, but I'll track down
the rest. The thing that clinches it, though, is this Chapin character. He used to work for the law firm Harley
has on retainer, although he didn't handle Harley himself. I don't know why no one looked into Chapin's
background before this. The connection is pretty ob-
vious, but that's show biz," she concluded breezily.

"That's great news," O'Mara said unenthusiasti-
cally.

"You seem real excited," she returned wryly. "I call
to tell you about the sports journalism coup of the decade, and you sound like I'm the vet with bad news
about your dog."

"Sorry," he apologized. "Harley isn't the kind of man
I get along with well. Nothing panned out with the
ballet company, huh?"

"Nope. I did try to find out something about the
Charles's finances, but it was like trying to break into
Fort Knox. People that rich are very discreet, O'Mara.
Besides, what would she want with a football team?
She's already up to her eyeballs with her ballet com-
pany."

"I suppose so." So he'd been a prize jerk, after all.
"Well, thanks a lot, Pringle. I owe you one."

"I'm sorry if the truth is disappointing."

"It's not that it's disappointing, just hard to face." He
said good-night to Pringle and put the phone down.

I've hurt someone I was really starting to care about, he thought as he paced up and down the living room. *Maybe it's because I was having such strong feelings about her that I grabbed at any reason to pull back.* It wouldn't be the first time he'd done that. Sure, he'd had his fantasies about settling down on the farm with a wife and kids, but every time he'd come remotely close to making the dream come true he'd backed off. Accusing Jo of manipulating him for the owner was one of his more compelling excuses.

He thought about that for a long time, thought about how he'd like to try to make a go of it with her. She was really special. Not only was she beautiful and sexy, she was funny and feisty. It had taken a lot of gumption to stand up to him that morning. His size made him a formidable character, but his black Irish temper had scared off men twice her size. She was quite a woman, was Jo. And he had a lot of making up to do.

He seized the phone and punched in her number, but all he got on her line was endless ringing. He called her at every opportunity over the weekend, but she never answered. She was either at the theater eighteen hours a day, he figured, or she'd unplugged the phone—or both.

On Monday the hours passed slowly until it was at last time to dress for the opening. He shined his best shoes until he could use them for mirrors, brushed the dark blue suit he kept for very special occasions, donned his favorite silk shirt, the pale blue one with the thin red stripe, spent a long time making the perfect knot in his wine-red silk tie. Clean handkerchief in breast pocket, a splash of cologne, one final combing of his just-cut hair, and he was ready to go.

He hardly recognized himself as he took a last look in the mirror. But it wasn't his clothes or the careful grooming that arrested him; it was the look in his eyes. It took him a long time to name the quality he saw there. He'd seen it only on rare occasions. It was called humility.

10

Jo STOOD IN THE WINGS awaiting her entrance in *Birdland.* She pointed, then flexed her toes, checked the ribbons on her shoes, made several unnecessary adjustments to her costume, repositioned the pins in her hair. The more she fiddled and fussed the less she had to think about how nervous she was. The more she could avoid feeling the churning in the pit of her stomach.

The familiar ballet was the first on the program, but her anxiety was not over dancing it. If only Sasha's ballet was first she wouldn't have to spend the entire night feeling this way. But after *Birdland* she'd have two other ballets and three intermissions to get through before the debut of the new work. It seemed an eternity.

And then there was the problem of what would happen after the performance. Would O'Mara show up at the party? Would he bring a date? Would he talk to her? Ignore her? Her anxiety about it was so great that she had thought about not attending the party. But she couldn't do that. Not even if she made a fool of herself in Sasha's ballet. She'd have to show up and appear to be having a good time, no matter what.

Sasha joined her in the wings and nodded curtly. Usually there would have been a stream of whispered endearments, a hug, a kiss on the hand or cheek or mouth, but even the unflappable Trevetsky was tense tonight. It wasn't only nerves that kept the two dancers from their usual preperformance exchange. The relationship between them had grown more and more strained during the final days of rehearsal. After the dress rehearsal Sasha had said cruel and inexcusable things to her about her talent, her technique, his choice of her to star in his ballet. Jo had responded in kind. The gossip mills would be turning for months on the fuel she and Sasha had fed them.

They awaited their entrance cue tautly, not looking at one another. Once on stage their professionalism took over, and they danced as if they were the best of friends, the most loving of partners. The sound of the applause that followed their duet indicated they had concealed their true feelings from the audience. Backstage the icy conditions prevailed.

Between ballets the dancers usually played cards, knitted leg warmers, read books or chatted, but because it was opening night feelings were running too high for such mundane activities. Jo missed them sorely and longed for the boredom that usually prevailed backstage. She passed the time pacing, doing exercises to keep her muscles supple. And worrying.

She couldn't remember being so nervous before a performance, not before her first appearance as a soloist with the company, not even before her audition to join the company. She just wanted the performance to be over. Standing in the wings, she wished it was possible to hurry things along, the way a thirty-three and a third rpm record could be played at seventy-eight rpm's. Even so, her cue came too quickly, and she was onstage.

Alone. In the spotlight. After a single, terrifying second she responded instinctively. The memories of the body-crushing work, the friction with Sasha, the worries about O'Mara fell away. She became a vehicle for pure energy, pure movement. She danced. She was dance. And she triumphed.

Bouquet upon bouquet of flowers rained down on her at the curtain call. The moment was one she had dreamed of all her life, made all the more sweet by coming when she had least expected it. Sasha joined her onstage. He took her hand and kissed it gallantly. The audience applauded wildly, and more flowers fell on both of them. She bowed once more and turned to bow to him, to thank him for creating such a ballet for her. The smile he beamed at her was genuine. She had done well. All was forgiven.

In the wings, the company crowded around them, and there was much hugging and kissing. Finally Jo and Sasha broke away to her dressing room. She dropped her arm load of flowers, some crushed now from the embraces of her colleagues, on the dressing table and collapsed in the chair. She was suddenly overwhelmingly tired, not exhausted and down as she'd been, but wonderfully drained and empty.

Sasha leaned against the dressing table and smiled impishly. "So we have done it, eh, my love?"

"No thanks to you," she said good-naturedly. He opened his mouth to protest, but she stopped him. "And don't give me any of that stuff about how you were egging me on so I'd perform better. I wouldn't believe it for a minute." She let out a long, happy sigh and propped her feet on the table. She bent over to unlace her toe shoes, and Sasha came around behind her. He put one hand on her shoulder and lifted her face to the mirror.

"This has been an important night for me, for us," he said to their reflection. "I saw you as if I've never seen you before. We can become a partnership like no other, Jo." He rested his chin on the top of her head, still looking at her through the mirror. "We are a better match than you and the 'dark man of the Empire.'" He drew his hand lightly across her mouth when she began to speak. "What does he know of dancing, of dancers, of the life we lead?"

Of dancing, more than you'd imagine, she thought, remembering how fluid he had been at Neptune. And after. She took off her toe shoes and put them on the dressing table. "Sasha, I know you mean every word you're saying right this minute. But in half an hour—" She dropped her feet to the floor, turned and smiled fondly at him. He would always be rash and impetuous, but without those special qualities he wouldn't be the great dancer or the fine choreographer he was. She stood and raised her hand to pat his cheek, but he caught her hand in a strong grip and pressed the palm to his lips. "Sasha," she cautioned, and withdrew her hand. "Get out of here, so I can get dressed."

He pouted. "Only if you insist."

"I do," she said firmly, and shooed him to the door.

"All right," he relented. "I will wait for you. We must arrive at Suzanne's together. Arm in arm. So will we leave, as well. You will come to your senses." He took her hand and kissed it, looking up at her with an appealing mixture of pleading and the conviction that he could not be refused.

A hundred women would happily relinquish their eye teeth to be standing here in my tights, Jo thought. But all she could think of was whether or not O'Mara would show up at the party. "How you can be so conceited and so charming at the same time, I'll never figure out." She took her hand back and pushed him toward the door.

"It is the secret of my success."

"Out!" she said with a laugh.

She took her time getting out of her costume and into a dressing gown. Sasha would no doubt want to make an entrance at Mrs. Charles's. He was the only one in the company who dared to call her Suzanne. But that was Sasha, treading where others would not dare. Who else, after the way he had treated her for the past couple of weeks, would walk in here and proposition her? She could imagine his behavior if his ballet had not been a success. He would have blamed it on her, railed at her, reviled her. It would not have been a pleasant scene. But even though she knew that about him, a part of her wanted to believe in the possibility of a relationship with him. For he had touched the truth with his words. What did O'Mara, even if they could patch things up, know of her life, of its rigors and discipline? No, better to forget him, concentrate on building her reputation and stature as a dancer.

Unfortunately, she thought as she creamed off her heavy stage makeup, that wouldn't keep her warm on a winter night or be very good company in twenty years' time, when her dancing days were far behind her.

She showered and then slipped into shimmering hose and an ivory charmeuse teddy. Her ivory silk crepe dress sat loosely on her shoulders, then fell in soft pleats to a gathered drop waist accentuated by a band of iridescent beading. The skirt floated to midcalf, with a slit on the right side that revealed her shapely legs when she walked. She gathered her hair into a ponytail high on the left side of her head, wound a band of ivory silk around the fastening and let the ends of it mingle with her dark hair. She wore dangling, carved ivory earrings and a row of twisted ivory bangles on each wrist.

Satisfied with the effect—she looked every inch the stylish and successful artiste—she picked up her handwoven woolen shawl and left the dressing room. She could tell from the quiet in the hall that most of the dancers had left for the party. Sasha was chatting with the security guard at the end of the hallway and didn't notice her at first. But at the sound of her heels clicking on the tiles, he whirled and sped to her, lavishing praise with every step. She had never looked more beautiful, more confident, more the prima ballerina.

He led her to the limousine waiting at the stage door, proclaiming that now that she was going to be a star, she must be draped in furs. He would buy her a magnificent sable coat the next day. She must let him do that for her.

Sasha had become an American in so many ways but had retained his Russian love of furs. In winter he sported an enormous sable hat, and his most favored ladies had been wrapped in Russian sable. But Jo preferred not to warm herself with garments many animals had given their lives for. She refused his offer gently and turned the conversation to the performance. With his photographic memory for movement, Sasha began to recount each step, and soon the offer to buy her a sable coat was ancient history. *He's as precise as an instant replay tape of a football game*, she thought as she listened to him dissect every movement. The thought made her realize how easily and how often her mind strayed to anything that even remotely concerned O'Mara.

The party didn't come to an immediate halt when she and Sasha entered Mrs. Charles's living room. It took a few moments for the animated party goers to realize they'd arrived. Then suddenly there was a hush. Mrs. Charles swept across the fifty-foot room to them, and a thunderous burst of applause was unleashed. Jo felt it physically. It was like wading into the sea, eyes fixed on the horizon, and meeting an unexpected wave. Her grip on Sasha's arm tightened when she saw O'Mara at the far end of the room, staring at her, not clapping, not smiling, his gaze so penetrating she felt it boring into her even at this distance.

The crowd that formed around them cut him off from view, but she was keenly aware of his presence even as she accepted embraces and compliments from a steady stream of well-wishers—the company's most important supporters, dance critics, Empire team members, celebrities from other areas of the performing arts. She was handed a flute of champagne, fed crackers topped with caviar and crumbled egg. She was, in short, lionized. And she loved it. Not that she could make it a life's pursuit like Sasha, but she finally understood why he reached for it at every opportunity. She felt as if the world turned on her axle, that she controlled its speed and the degree of movement effortlessly, as easily as lifting a finger.

But even as she laughed and joked and hugged and was hugged, she was aware of the one person in the room who did not move in her direction. He stayed in one spot, chatted with those who happened by him but made no effort to join in the merrymaking. Gradually the crowd around her and Sasha dispersed, and she was left chatting with Sara Wilson, who covered dance for the *Village Voice*. Rory Washington and his wife, Wanda, moved in after Sara was pulled away by someone else.

"We'd already bought two tickets," Rory said after lavishing Jo with praise, "so our daughter, Toinette, and Wanda's younger sister came with us on the freebies. Then O'Mara gave us his extra ticket, so Toinette invited a school friend, too. They're spending the night with Wanda's sister while the old folks go out and party."

"The girls will remember this all their lives," Wanda put in. "They're eight and can't decide if they want to be ballerinas or police officers. I'll bet ballerina will be top of the list for the next month or so."

Jo laughed along with the Washingtons, but her thoughts were on O'Mara. Though he'd been standing alone all evening, her heart still fluttered at the knowledge that he'd planned to come by himself. She chatted with Rory and Wanda, her mind only half on the conversation. She needed to get away and think for a few minutes. Were they going to eye each other across the room all night, or come together and talk like civilized adults? When she could politely do so, she excused herself and made her way, slowly and with many stops, toward the powder room. It was occupied when she got there, but she couldn't stay in there for very long, anyway. Where else could she go? Over the years she had been to many parties at Mrs. Charles's. She thought she remembered a small study at the end of the hall beyond the powder room and went off to find it.

O'Mara watched her leave the room, as he had watched her every move that night. Probably gone to powder her nose, he thought. Well, at least she'd gotten away from the Russian wolfhound. He had wanted to go to her himself from the moment she'd come into the room, but there was no way he was going to compete for her attention. *Who are you kidding, O'Mara,* he asked himself. *You could easily have gone over while she was talking to Rory and Wanda, and you stood here like a bump on a log.* Well, maybe not like a bump on a log. Bumps couldn't have the feelings he'd been having.

Watching her dance had been a revelation. He'd known from seeing her in class that she was good, but he hadn't imagined just how good she was. She was transcendent; everyone else on the stage had looked dull compared to her. Even in the first ballet, when she hadn't been quite as splendid as in her solo, she'd held her ground with the Russian. And that guy had charisma onstage like O'Mara had never seen. Still, little Jo, his Jo, had given the guy a run for his money. He was proud of her, even if he had to give Trevetsky his due. But he was still jealous. Not so much because Trevetsky had touched her while O'Mara was sitting miles away in the audience, but because she seemed to be enjoying his company so much at the party. She'd let him hang all over her, had put her arm through his a hundred times—but who was counting?

Hell's bells, he thoughts, *I can turn it on as heavily as that Russian wolf in wolf's clothing.* He moved across the room to meet Jo as she returned from the powder room, running interference like the pro he was. He positioned himself by the door to the hallway, thinking of all the devastatingly charming things he would say to her when she came back. But she didn't come back. He waited and waited and then decided to go looking for her.

The powder-room door was closed when he went past and just in case she was still there, he stationed himself outside it. He leaned nonchalantly against the wall, hands in pockets, one foot crossed in front of the other, mouth arranged in a calculatingly sure smile. It was hard not to feel foolish when the woman who emerged from the room wasn't Jo. He knew she hadn't returned to the party. In the main room he could hear that the combo had stopped playing, and a man was banging minor chords on the piano and singling loudly in Russian. Others were clapping hands and shouting encouragement. Trevetsky must be putting on a side-show. When he found Jo, at least she wouldn't be in a clinch with the wolfhound, O'Mara thought with some small satisfaction.

He continued down the hall and came to a small book-lined room at the end of it. Jo was standing in front of the window looking out. Even with her back to him, he was overwhelmed by her beauty. He easily imagined the soft curves of her body beneath the soft folds of her dress. Her long neck was inspiringly elegant; the silk strands in her hair emphasized its dark richness. All the swagger went out of him. The charming remarks, the sweep-her-off-her-feet routines he had planned sounded phony and tasteless as they raced through and out of his brain. He greeted her with a simple, modest hello.

Jo turned slowly at the sound of his voice. Silently she rejoiced because he had sought her out. She didn't have to think any more about what to do about him when she went back to the party. "Hello," she said quietly.

"I wanted to talk to you." He took a step into the room.

"Did you?" Her heart was beating as furiously as it had at the rising of the curtain that night.

He took another step toward her. He wanted to run to her, take her in his arms, hold her ever so close, but he told himself to stop acting like an overeager colt and move slowly. He wasn't good at apologies, but the most gracious one he had ever made came pouring out of his mouth. "I got it all wrong. I don't know how, I'm not sure why, even after all the thinking I've done about it, but I didn't do well by you, Jo. Worst of all, I didn't do well by us."

"Is there an 'us'?" she had to ask.

"If you want there to be. If you can forgive me."

Alone with O'Mara, she wondered how, even for the few seconds that it had crossed her mind, she could ever have considered a liaison with Sasha. Even a less impossible Sasha, if such a creature had existed. Maybe O'Mara didn't know anything about her world, but when he looked at her that way, she saw that he knew her. Maybe he did have the hottest temper this side of Hades, but he could make a heavenly apology. "Where do we start?"

"By letting me tell you how wonderful you were tonight. I didn't know how magnificent you could be until I saw you. I—"

She saw how serious he was, how much he wanted
to tell her he'd enjoyed the performance, but she'd had
enough heroine worship for the evening. Besides, that
wasn't what she and O'Mara were about. They weren't
a mutual admiration society. She held up a hand and
stopped him with a weary grin. "Please, O'Mara, could
you tell me something else? I've been hearing that all
night."

He looked dumbfounded for a moment and then
burst out laughing. He knew just how she felt. Sometimes after he'd made a spectacular play, he got tired of
having people clap him on the back, tired of having
them run through the play over and over again. "Okay,
what do you want to know?"

"Um . . ." She thought for a moment. "Did you win
yesterday? I haven't had a minute to look at the papers."

"We lost a close one," he said with a philosophical
shrug. He hadn't been at his best. "My judgment wasn't
as sharp as it could have been." He looked at her keenly.
"My attention kept wandering."

"I see," she said. The way he was gazing at her gave
her a pretty good idea about where his attention had
been.

"Come here," he said. "I'll show you some of the
plays." There was a small table in the corner set up for
chess. He picked eleven of the pieces to represent each
team and set them up in line-of-scrimmage formation.
They both leaned over the table, and he began to move
the pieces to illustrate the crucial play of the first quarter. The play hadn't been the least bit amusing when it
had happened, but as he showed to Jo how the other
team had pulled a brilliant quarterback sack on him,

he began to see the funny side of it. Soon they were both chuckling about how he'd been taken unawares.

Even as she experienced it, Jo marveled as she had on other occasions at how easily they could come together. Not a quarter of an hour before they had been separated by what seemed like miles and miles of Mrs. Charles's Persian bijar carpet. And here they were playing "Monday-night quarterback" with each other as if nothing could be more natural. Of course, there were a lot of things that needed to be said, but that would happen in its own time.

O'Mara was setting up the pieces for another play when one of Jo's colleagues swept into the room. "There you are, Jo," she exclaimed. "Everyone's been looking for you. Sasha's started singing, and you're missing all the fun." She stopped to draw a breath and looked from Jo to O'Mara and back. "Well, maybe not." She winked at Jo and started to back out of the room. "I'll tell Sasha I couldn't find you."

O'Mara stopped moving the pieces around on the table. "Will he come looking for you?"

Jo listened and heard that Sasha was still holding forth at the piano. He'd gone from the lively Russian songs to the mournful ones. There would be no stopping him now. He would sing till dawn if anyone would listen. "Are you kidding? He's got an audience. He won't leave until they do."

He turned back to his chess pieces, but the desire to rehash the game had waned. He wanted to be alone with her, in a room where no one could barge in, where they could talk, touch, kiss, feel. He put down the knight he was holding and touched a finger tentatively to her cheek. "There's something I'd very much like to show you. Will you come with me?"

"Where?" she asked shakily.

"To see my farm."

"It'll be the middle of the night when we get there."

"Only the middle, not the end."

She hesitated, not because she didn't want to go with him, but she had other commitments. "I have class in the morning and a rehearsal at two."

He moved closer and lifted her chin with his hand. "There's lots of empty rooms in the farmhouse where you can warm up. I'll give you a chair to hold on to instead of a *barre* in the morning. I'll even hold the chair for you."

"Don't you have practice tomorrow morning?" she asked unsteadily. His breath was warm and sweet on her face. She held on to the edge of the table for support.

"Since Mrs. Charles canceled class at the Metropolitan, I talked the coach into a morning off, seeing as how it would be 'the morning after' for a lot of guys." He folded her into her arms. She was as neat a package as he could ever hope to hold. He combed his fingers through her silken ponytail. "Let's face it," he said to the top of her head, "we've both run out of excuses."

He was right. She had no evasions left to offer.

11

THEY LEFT THE PARTY quietly, without returning to the main room, took a cab to O'Mara's garage and soon were speeding up the East Side highway on their way north.

"I've never left an opening night party before the reviews were out," Jo said wistfully. It seemed funny to be doing so on the biggest night of her career.

"We can go back," O'Mara offered.

"No. The reviews will read the same tomorrow afternoon."

"All raves, no doubt. For you, that is. I don't know about the rest."

"I don't seem to care so much what they say this time. I know I danced well. I know the audience loved Sasha's piece." She was silent for a moment, thinking. "I guess what it boils down to is that I feel like I've proved myself tonight. I don't have to go out there and do it over and over and over. Now all I have to do is dance." O'Mara didn't say anything, but she knew he was listening to her, hearing her, heeding her. "The last couple of weeks have been tough—too much to do, Sasha snapping at my heels like a hungry crocodile."

"And what I did to you couldn't have helped. Especially when you had to see me twice a week whether you liked it or not."

"Your timing could have been better," she conceded wryly. "When I stood in the wings tonight, I thought I couldn't do it. I couldn't remember what the music sounded like, couldn't remember the first step, but suddenly I was out there in the spotlight. It was as if the stage lights were connected to some switch inside me, some inner light. Once it was turned on I could see exactly where I was going, and I went. It was that simple."

O'Mara took one hand off the steering wheel and let it rest lightly on her knee. "That was what was so amazing to me, how easy you made it look. There was that eerie music I could hardly make sense of, all those contortions you were doing with your body, and you made it look beautiful and effortless." He brushed the back of his hand over her thigh. "The rest can be that easy, Jo. We can be that easy, too."

"Can we?" she asked, trying to keep her teeth from chattering. When he touched her, her body felt as if it were connected to a live electrical wire. His hand inched up her thigh, and she breathed in sharply. "Drive," she said huskily.

"I am driving," he answered, moving his hand to the top of her thigh.

"With both hands, O'Mara," she said tautly. He let his fingers trail back to her knee. She picked up his hand and put it back on the wheel.

He picked up speed. "We'll just have to get there sooner, then."

She rearranged her skirt and commanded her stomach to stop fluttering. "It's funny," she said thoughtfully. "Here we are running away together to your farm in the middle of the night, and there are so many things I don't know about you."

"Like what?"

The subject of his name popped into her head, ahead of all the other questions. "Like why I can't call you Fred, for instance."

"Can't you pick something else?" he asked testily.

"I will, but first tell me why you don't like being called Fr—"

"Don't say it again, Jo," he interrupted. "I'm easily provoked."

"You can say that again!"

"All right," he relented. He didn't want to keep secrets from her, but he didn't like talking about his name. It made him think about home, made him remember too much. "Promise you won't laugh."

"I promise." There was a long pause. "I'm waiting," she added sweetly.

"Me sainted muther," he said with a phony Irish brogue, trying to make a joke out of it, "named me after— Aargh!" He dropped the brogue. "I can hardly say it out loud."

"No one else will hear you."

"She named me after a dog," he spat out.

Jo couldn't help herself. She tried everything, holding her hands over her mouth, over her stomach, holding her breath, but the laughter burbled out of her, anyway. "I'm sorry. That's awful. What kind of dog?" she got out before another outburst overtook her.

"A setter." He practically growled himself. "An Irish setter. Can you imagine how I felt as a kid when I found out? I had never liked my name, so once when I was about twelve or so I asked my mother about it. I figured if I was named after some famous person I might like it better. Ha!"

"Your mother must have thought very highly of the dog," she deadpanned.

"That's what she told me. That the dog had been her best friend when she was a girl, so it was like being named after her best friend. Maybe I might not have have minded a horse. A horse is noble. But a dog." He shook his head slowly from side to side.

"You know what your trouble is? You hang on to things for too long. You don't let go of what makes you angry. You take it in, nurse it, feed it, care for it. And then you're surprised when it grows. You can't have it both ways, O'Mara."

He shifted his eyes briefly from the road to her. He'd never thought about it that way before, but she was right. He'd been carrying around this thing about his name since he was twelve years old. "You might have something there," he allowed. "I'm doing the same thing with the owner," he realized after a moment. "Aren't I?"

"That or a pretty good imitation."

"You knock me out, Jo. Not only gorgeous and talented and sexy, but smart, too." He tugged playfully on her ponytail. "You've got some good gray matter under here."

His hand dropped back onto the steering wheel. Jo's entire scalp tingled as if she'd had a massage. Hair might not be living matter, but it was a terrific conductor of electricity. She settled back into the Jag's luxurious leather seat, felt the powerful motor carrying them along as steadily as a river current. "Are we there yet?" she asked dreamily.

"We're getting there, Jo, we're getting there." There was no masking the excitement or impatience in his voice. He wanted to show her the farm, the house, wanted to feel her warmth in the mostly empty rooms. In the morning they'd go out to the barn; he'd introduce her to his horses. Then they'd have a big breakfast. Of what, he asked himself. There was an all-night supermarket on the way. They'd stop there for provisions. He was so lost in thought, the sound of her voice surprised him. He didn't take in what she had said and asked her to repeat it.

"I said your mother sounds like a very interesting woman."

"They don't make 'em like her anymore, that's for sure."

"Tell me about her. And about your family."

He told her about the dairy farm far upstate near the Canadian border where he'd grown up. That was the easy part, describing the house and the barn, the pastures, the river where he'd fished in summer. But once he set the scene he knew he had to let the drama unfold. Jo hadn't asked him for a travelog.

"My mother ran it herself and raised four kids on her own after my father faded away. I was about ten then; my older brother was twelve. The twins—my sisters—weren't in school yet."

"What do you mean, your father faded away?" Jo found his choice of words odd.

"Well, he was one of those people who always seem to be wrapped up in their own world. He was around—I can remember him teaching me how to milk, how to fix things, stuff like that—but he never seemed to be really 'there.' I sensed that in the way kids do, but I couldn't explain it then. Now I see that he couldn't handle the responsibility for making the farm run, for being a husband and a father. The tougher things got on the farm, the more distant he became. Finally, when I was about seven or eight, he started disappearing. Physically. First he'd go for just a day or two at a time, then it was a week or two, then two weeks became a month. When he came back he never said where he'd been or why he'd gone. He'd show up at the door and act as if he'd been in town for a few hours. After us kids had gone to bed, I'd hear my mother asking him where he'd been, but he never said anything.

"I don't know why he kept going and coming back. Guilt maybe. Or hope that everything had changed while he was away. But it didn't work out that way. He'd come back to more of the same. Or worse. He said less and less each time he came back. I remember my sisters had this book of poems. There was one I used to read them, about a kid who lost his shadow. It was like my father was just the opposite. His shadow was there, but the real him was somewhere else.

"Sometimes it was weird. I'd find him in the barn or out in a field, just standing there like a statue, frozen right in the middle of doing something. When you talked to him then, he took a real long time to move or to answer. Sometimes he didn't move or answer at all.

"Then one day he must have realized that nothing was going to change. Any guilt or responsibility he felt must have been gone. He left and never came back. We never knew what happened to him. We still don't." He stopped talking. He'd said enough, more than he'd ever said to anyone about his father, even to Rory. He liked the way Jo wasn't falling all over herself to offer him sympathy. She knew when and how to listen. He took her hand and squeezed it lightly before he continued.

"My brother runs the farm now, lives in the old house. I had a new place built for my mother on the property, no stairs, all the modern conveniences. She's got arthritis pretty bad from milking on all those cold mornings, but she still does her share. I'd like to see anybody try and stop her."

"Do you ever think about your father?" she asked quietly. His story had affected her deeply. She tried to imagine not knowing where one of her parents was, or even if they were dead or alive, but in her mind, as in life, they were planted firmly in their snug, suburban home.

"Sometimes," he admitted. "I still have this fantasy that he's out there somewhere, that one day he'll show up at the stadium after a game. Maybe that's why I had to become famous at something. To give my father a chance to find me. But I've been a pro for ten years, and he hasn't shown up. I don't think he's going to."

"I'm sorry," Jo said very softly.

"It's not your fault." His response was gruff.

"I didn't say it was, but I'm still sorry your dream didn't come true."

"It's an old dream, Jo. I hardly ever have it anymore. Let's concentrate on new dreams. The ones that *are* going to come true."

He reached for her hand and brought it gently to his lips. He held it there for a moment, and she felt that time had stopped for an instant, then carried on in a new direction, still linear, but pointing the way to a new, different time for them.

They drove on silently, and Jo thought about the story he'd told her. It explained so much about him, why the man whose heart was in raising horses had spent a decade as a pro football player. It explained the anger that was in him and why he held on to things so tightly. It helped her understand why she had fallen so hard for him. There was more to him than met the eye, more to him than he let show. He wasn't just an egotistical jock, even though he could give an Academy Award-winning performance in the role. But she had known that all along, or almost all along.

The touch of his hand on her knee once again cut off her thoughts. He drew his fingers up her thigh, up the side of her body to her face. "Are we there yet?" she asked in a small, shaky voice. She didn't know how many of these touches her system could take without fulfillment of the promises they offered.

"Almost. There's one stop we need to make." Shortly after that they turned off the highway and onto a local shopping road, the kind found in every suburban community, with a strip of shopping centers, gas stations, supermarkets. He signaled and pulled into the parking lot of a market whose neon sign beckoned customers twenty-four hours a day.

In their fancy clothes, Jo and O'Mara were a sharp contrast to the rest of the store's patrons, weary mothers in jeans and jackets shopping after working a night shift or putting the kids to bed, a pair of firemen buying for the station house, a raucous gang of young men getting beer and chips for a late-night poker or gab fest. They garnered a few odd looks, but they didn't mind as they stocked up on breakfast food, discussing the relative merits of orange over grapefruit juice, getting to know each other's likes and dislikes.

With each passing minute Jo felt she knew O'Mara better and better. And the more she knew the more she left behind her own world and entered the one they were creating together. When they'd chosen and paid for their groceries, he hefted the sack in one arm, and she linked her arm through the other. He smiled at her, and she rested her head against his warm, substantial shoulder as they walked back to the car.

Ah, this is the life, O'Mara thought as he put the groceries on the back seat of the Jag and handed Jo into the front. *Going home together after a night out, knowing we'll wake up together, anticipating the joys that will come before morning.* He couldn't remember ever having felt the curious mixture of serenity and excitement he was feeling now. This is what it might feel like at the beginning of a race, when you were somehow sure your horse was going to win.

"Only another ten minutes," he told her as he started up the car. Before shifting into gear and pulling out, he turned to her and took her face in his hands. Very gently he bestowed a kiss on her lips. "Usually when I come up here I drive like crazy, hardly thinking about anything except getting here. But this trip, Jo, this trip has been different. It was as if I was already where I wanted to be, just because you were in the car with me." He nibbled on her lips and caressed her neck. "Even though there were so many ways I wanted to touch you," he murmured as his hands roved lightly over breasts, her waist, her hips. "And couldn't," he whispered with undisguised longing.

Her heart pumped as if to send jets of cooling water through her inflamed body. He explored her lips with his, parted them with his searching tongue, found the warm, willing, waiting wetness of her mouth. When he released her they were both breathing hard; the windows of the car were steamy. "Whoever said necking in cars was for teenagers only?" He took her hand and pressed it to his pounding heart. "Lord, Jo, you make me feel like one."

"I feel as giddy as a girl at her first dance," she admitted with a giggle.

"Let's go home," he murmured huskily. He depressed the clutch, shifted into first and peeled out of the parking space.

"You're not just feeling like a teenager, you're driving like one," she said as she held on to her seat. Her head was reeling the way it would have if she'd done a series of turns without spotting. And she'd learned to spot when she was eight. She was going back in time, losing lifelong restraints and conditioning, experiencing life anew with him. It was wonderful, marvelous, exhilarating.

"And I'm going to sing like a teenager, too." He launched into an exuberant rendition of a golden oldie. She clapped along with him, feeling gay and childlike and perfectly happy.

They quieted down when they turned away from the neon-lighted street. They couldn't sing and carry on when the road they traveled was utterly quiet, utterly deserted, the darkness pierced only by the gleam of white corral fencing that undulated in gentle waves across the rolling land.

"It's so peaceful here," she whispered. She came so little into real countryside like this that the contrast to her normal nighttime habitat surprised her. The sky was a dark, dark blue, not the limp lavender that passed for night in the city. The stars shone clearly, in great numbers and traceable patterns.

"Mmm," he answered, unwilling to intrude on the quiet or break the spell that was winding around them like silken thread.

The driveway to O'Mara's farm was a long corridor lined with rows of white corral fencing. Though she could see in the dim moonlight that it was only a simple farmhouse that they approached, she felt like a queen on the way to a lavish castle.

He pulled up in front of the house and helped her out of the car. He held her hand tightly as they stepped up to the porch, didn't let her go as he took out the key and opened the door. They exchanged an emotion-charged glance and stepped into the house together. He faced her, taking her hands in his. "Welcome," he said, looking deeply into her eyes, speaking volumes with one word.

She shivered involuntarily. She had never felt so fully wanted in her life, not even during the curtain calls earlier that night, not in the loving and supportive home where she had grown up. This was a different kind of wanting and acceptance, as if he were putting his life into her hands but relieving her of any weight that might go along with his trust.

He held her close, warming her with his embrace. "Let's go upstairs and light a fire." He switched on the hall light, and they climbed the stairs, arms wrapped around each other's waists. The room he led her to had a massive stone fireplace on the outside wall. There was a thick, colorful rag rug on the hearth and a single chair facing the fire. He seated her in it, bending to brush his lips across her neck. "We'll have to get another chair for the fireside. Very soon."

He shed his suit jacket and loosened his tie before gathering kindling and applying a match to it. When the fire was going strong, he piled on an armful of logs. Flames rose and crackled, burned in blues and reds and yellows. "They look the way I feel," she said to him wonderingly.

"You and me both." He caressed her bare arm as he moved beside the chair. His hands went to her hair and began to unwind the silken cord that bound it. More than straight, dark waves of her hair were released when he freed it. Waves of passion rolled through each of them, one lapping over the next, creating a tidal wave of feeling. He fell to his knees in front of her chair. "Jo, Jo," he whispered.

"Yes," she responded, cradling his head in her lap, stroking his hair, bending to kiss the top of his head.

"Let me love you. Please." He sat back on his heels and held his hands out to her.

"Yes," she said again, and put her hands into his. She could do nothing else. The whole evening, every moment since they had met—good times and bad—had been leading them to this place.

As one person they rose and stepped away from the chair. "The fire will keep us warm," he said, brushing an unruly strand of hair from her face. He cupped her face in his hands and brought his lips to hers. Her arms closed around his back, and she felt the depth and breadth of him, the strength of him. His hands slid down over her shoulders and around her back. He crushed her to him, so close she could feel his heart beating against her chest.

The long, clinging kiss they shared left them breathing hard and fast. Panting lightly, he stepped back from her, ran his hands down her legs. "How do I get you out of this gorgeous piece of silk?"

"You slip it up and over my head," she said in a quavering voice.

"Like this?" He reached under the skirt of her dress and drew the fabric up to her hips, slowly caressing the outside of her legs.

"Yes," she whispered.

He slipped his fingers beneath the dropped waistband and continued to raise the silk over her body. His fingers were as warm and soft as the material, and she was caressed twice over. She lowered her head and straightened her arms in front of her as he pulled the wisp of fabric up and over her head. He gazed at her in the charmeuse teddy, filling his eyes with her. "I do love sexy underwear," he said hoarsely.

Her nipples stiffened as he grazed her breasts with the back of his hand. Her stomach plummeted, then resurged when she felt the heat of his hand through the flimsy material. He touched her intimately, and she quivered and put her hands on his arms to steady herself. "I didn't know lingerie could produce an effect like this."

"Neither did I." Holding on to her with one arm, he moved around her, gazing at her with admiration. He laid her dress carefully on the back of the chair and reached for his tie.

"No, let me." His hands fell readily to his sides, and she unknotted the tie and drew it from under his collar. She placed it on top of her dress. Standing closer to him, she unbuttoned his shirt, opened it to reveal his magnificent chest. She pressed her body to his as she slid the shirt over his shoulders. He shuddered when the silk of her teddy met his naked flesh. Her hands raced to unfasten his belt. He stepped quickly out of his trousers, shoes and socks. "Talk about sexy underwear," she breathed, eyeing the narrow swath of black that barely covered him.

They circled each other in a slow dance, one as ancient as man and woman and desire, moving closer and closer until they were fast in each other's arms. His hands roved her body, coming to rest between her legs. He unsnapped her teddy, dropped to his knees and followed the garment with his lips as he drew it up past her hips, her waist, her breasts. He stood and pulled the teddy over her head, letting it float silently to the floor. He bent his head to take a nipple into his mouth, sucked at it, flicked it with his tongue as he drew her shimmering hose down over her shaking legs.

He planted kisses all over her body as he followed the hose to the floor, helping her step out of her shoes and the stockings and pushing them aside. "You are so beautiful, Jo, so very, very beautiful," he said as his eyes took her in once more, from toe to top of head.

She tugged at his briefs, and they were quickly on the floor beside the rest of their discarded clothing. "I don't suppose I ought to tell a man he's beautiful, but you are."

"I don't mind hearing you say that. Not one bit . . . I feel like a new man."

He coaxed her down to the floor with him, his mouth fastened to hers. The rug had been warmed by the fire and cushioned their eager bodies as they rocked in each other's arms, tongues toying with kiss-swollen lips, hands exploring flame-hot skin. With his strong arms he lifted her easily to rest on top of him, chest to chest. She felt him hard and ready beneath her, sighing giddily as he reached between her legs and guided himself into her. He filled her, fulfilled her totally.

He fondled her breasts as he reached higher and higher inside her with each stroke. He varied their rhythm with unpredictable movements, leaving her a whimpering, trembling mass of sensation. She held on to his shoulders and settled down onto him. Suddenly he drove up into her, and she exploded with such ecstasy she felt she was being broken into two parts. At the same moment he grasped her buttocks; his body stiffened and then relaxed with a great shudder. They cried out together, and she fell on to his chest with a sob.

He stroked her hair, holding her very tightly with the other arm. "It's all right, my darling, it's all right," he whispered.

"I know," she whispered back.

"And it will always be all right," he promised.

They rested in each other's arms until the fire began to die, and there was a chill in the air. Then he carried her to the bed, tucked her under the covers and kissed her forehead. "I'll be right back. I have to bank the fire."

"Hurry," she said, and curled up in a contented ball, feeling like a well-fed cat about to cap off its feast with a delightful snooze in the sun. She was half dozing when he climbed into bed beside her. She snuggled up to him, and he took her in his arms. "Thank you for to-night," she murmured. "It was wonderful. Absolutely, positively wonderful." Her words trailed off as she sank into sleep.

"Yes," he said softly to her still form. "And thank you, Jo, for forgiving me, for coming with me tonight. I don't know what I've done to deserve you, but I pray I can keep doing it."

12

JO AWAKENED to a gentle shaking almost, it seemed, as soon as she'd fallen asleep. She hadn't felt O'Mara getting out of bed, but there he stood beside her, dressed in jeans and a plaid lumber jacket. "Wake up, sleepyhead," he said as he sat on the edge of the bed to caress her face. "You're missing the best part of the day."

"What time is it?" she mumbled.

"After seven already," he answered heartily.

"We can't have been asleep for more than a few hours," she complained.

"You can sleep on the way back to town." He held up some clothes. "Put these on. There are some boots by the kitchen door. I want you to see the horses. And then if you're very lucky, I'll cook you my special farmhouse breakfast."

She groaned and buried her head under her pillow.

"Uh-uh, none of that this morning. The sun is shining, the sky is bright blue, and there isn't a cloud in sight." He took her into his arms and a tight embrace.

She leaned against him like a rag doll and with great difficulty brought herself around. She lifted her face, and he kissed her so soundly that her waking process was more than complete. She pressed against him eagerly and ran her hands up and down his back in response.

He pulled himself away and held her at arm's length. "There's plenty of time for that after breakfast," he said firmly as he stood up. "But this morning won't wait." He plucked an enormous terry-cloth robe from the foot of the bed and held it out for her.

The robe engulfed her. She could have covered her head with the collar; the sleeves drooped way over the tips of her fingers, and the bottom dragged behind her like a train. But it smelled of him and felt lovely next to her skin, skin that still remembered his touch.

"You look very funny," he said fondly. "And very kissable."

He took her in his arms again for a warm, lingering kiss. Then he left the room, and she floated to the bathroom, clutching the pile of clothes he'd handed her. She showered quickly, reluctant to wash away the feel of him, but relieved as she toweled off to find that her body didn't easily relinquish its memory of last night's lovemaking.

She looked even more ridiculous in the clothes he'd found for her than she had in the robe. The white athletic socks reached to midcalf. She could pull the sweatpants up over her breasts and tie them like a strapless top. The sweatshirt covered halfway to her thighs. But the clothes were warm and comfortable, so she rolled up the sleeves and set about brushing her hair.

O'Mara stood at the kitchen window looking out at the grazing meadows, thinking for the hundredth time that morning that life was good and sweet beyond belief. He had slept for only a couple of hours. The dawn had wakened him and for a long time he had watched Jo sleeping, so long that the rhythm of his breathing had come to match hers. The thought had come to him then, as natural as their synchronized breathing. He loved her. He wanted to marry her. He wanted to wake up here with her every single morning. He wanted to watch her belly grow with their child, wanted to be with her and help it into the world.

He had held her, carefully so that she wouldn't wake, envisioning their life together. The days would unfold peacefully, quietly. They would stick close to home, loving each other and the farm more each day. It might take her some time to get used to living outside the city, to not spending most of her waking hours balanced on the tips of those crazy toe shoes. *You know*, he thought with a suppressed laugh, *she'll love it. Her feet will stop hurting for the first time in years.*

But what if she didn't want to give up dancing? He couldn't face the unbidden thought and quickly swept it aside. Hadn't she said last night that she'd reached the top, that she didn't have to go on proving herself anymore? She might as well go out with a bang. That would be a damned sight better than sticking around too long, trying to do things she couldn't anymore, making a fool of herself. Besides, dancing was so ephemeral. You couldn't hold on to it. Once the performance was over it was gone—forever. After last night, he knew he couldn't settle for anything less real and substantial than a total commitment. He didn't think Jo would, either.

He'd kissed her gently on the lips, then dressed and came downstairs to wait until he saw his manager, Nate Hempstead, moving about on the grounds. He'd been in the barn with Nate since then. He was certain Jo would come to love the place the way he did. She was used to an active life and would take well to the work here. *Funny,* he thought, *I don't even know if she can ride. If she can't, she can learn. I'll love teaching her.*

He turned from his reverie as he heard her padding down the back stairs. She smiled at him, still a bit sleepily, he thought, as she came into the kitchen. Then her eyes fell on the window and the view beyond, and ran over to it and to him.

"It's beautiful," she breathed, and took hold of his arm. The impact of the entire scene was tremendous, but surveying all its parts made it that much more exciting. A pair of colts were frisking at the top of the rise of the meadow, chasing each other, nudging one another with their noses, tails and manes flying. The trees on the horizon were poised between autumn and winter, some had leaves rippling in the breeze, others had assumed their spindly winter shapes. The grass had lost its high summer color to become a muted green background for the seemingly endless miles of white fencing.

"I knew you would love it," he said, and gave her a tight hug.

The boots waiting for her by the door were the only part of her outfit that fit reasonably well. "They belong to my manager's granddaughter," he explained. "She left them here this summer when she was visiting."

"Too bad she didn't leave a whole outfit."

"Nonsense. You look fabulous."

"If you don't mind the hobo look," she said with a grin.

He took her arm and opened the kitchen door. "Come on, seeing what's out there is much better than merely looking at it."

"Don't expect too much," she warned as they strode to the barn. "All I know about horses is what I read in *Black Beauty*, and that was a long time ago." She wasn't used to being around animals and was surprised by the smell in the barn. "Pungent," she remarked, and wrinkled her nose.

O'Mara laughed happily. "You'll get used to it. Pretty soon it'll smell better to you than all that fancy perfume you slather on yourself."

"Maybe," she said doubtfully as they stopped in front of the first stall.

"This is Bucephalus," he explained as he stroked the horse's nose and made soothing sounds. "Sire to the colts you saw out there and my favorite mount." They stopped at each box, and O'Mara told her about each horse. He spoke about them almost as he would have spoken about people.

"You know," she said as they strolled hand in hand around the meadow, "I think your second career is going to be even more successful than your first."

"I think so, too," he said, squeezing her hand. *But mostly because I'll have you with me,* he thought as he brought her hand to his lips and kissed the palm.

The fresh air awakened Jo's appetite, and she realized she'd eaten hardly anything the day before. She'd been too nervous before the performance, and she'd had only a few hors d'oeuvres at Mrs. Charles's. "Did you say something about feeding me before? I'm starving."

They went back to the house. O'Mara insisted she sit at the table and sip her juice while he made bacon and eggs, toast and coffee.

"This is great," Jo complimented him when she'd tucked in. The bacon was crisp, the eggs scrambled soft, the coffee strong and rich.

"Thanks. It's the best meal in my repertoire. Also the only meal in my repertoire."

"You're one meal ahead of me, then. The only thing I can make is salad, and that's only because you don't have to cook it."

"You must have a real domestic streak in you somewhere," he cajoled.

"None whatsoever," she announced proudly. "I'm useless in the kitchen and intend to remain so. Besides, I figure cooking is a liability for a dancer. It only encourages you to eat. I'd rather stick with salads and the occasional meal cooked by someone else."

Her words weren't exactly what O'Mara had expected to hear, but they didn't deter him from the course of action he'd determined earlier. That would be like switching plays after the ball was already in motion. Once the decision was made, they could make any adjustments they needed to make.

They finished their meal, and he poured them each a second cup of coffee. Jo looked around the kitchen as she sipped hers, thinking how nice it would be to know this place was here when her spirit needed rejuvenation. She began to imagine weekends here, after the season was over, of course. She was disciplined enough to give herself a class on a Sunday morning instead of joining the company. It would be lovely, waking up with him, taking long walks in the country. Maybe she would learn to ride, but only a very gentle, very old horse. She could break a leg—or worse—if she were thrown. Any injury, even a minor one, could cut precious years off a career.

Jo remembered with a start the previous evening's performance. It seemed as if it had happened in another life, but of course it hadn't. In fact, she had to go back and do it again tonight and the next night and the next. She glanced at the clock above the refrigerator. It was already after nine. "I guess we ought to leave pretty soon," she said sadly, reaching across the table for his hand.

"I thought you didn't have rehearsal until two o'clock."

"I don't, but I'd like to see the papers, have a little time to myself. It's been an action-packed twenty-four hours."

"More than that. It's changed my life, Jo. I want you to know how much." He moved his chair close to hers. "After the season is over I'm going to retire." Her mouth gaped, and she started to speak, but he silenced her with a finger on her lips. "I decided this morning. Sure, I could play a few more seasons, sock away some more dough, but I don't want to wait any longer. I want you to come here with me. I want us to run the place together. What do you say, Jo?"

"It sounds like a wonderful fantasy," she said, and let her head drop onto his shoulder.

"I'm not talking about fantasies. I'm talking about making them come true."

She sat up and looked at him closely. He was absolutely serious. "I know we had an incredible night last night. And I'd love to spend some time out here with

you. In fact, I was just thinking about how nice it would
be to spend the weekends with you here, after my season is over, of course."

He grasped her shoulders and said passionately, "I
don't want just the weekends. I want you here with me
all the time. I want to give you babies, Jo." He pressed
a hand to her belly.

Her stomach contracted at his touch, and she was
tempted for a second to forget everything else and say
yes to him. She might be able to live with that today,
but not for the rest of her life. She pushed his hand
away, reluctantly but gently. "Just because you're ready
to exchange one life you've known for another doesn't
mean I'm ready, too. Last night was the most important night of my career. I don't want to give it up now.
I can't give it up now."

"Why not? I know this is sudden, but once you get
used to the idea, I'm sure you'll see it my way. I love
you, Jo. Marry me. Stay with me. We could have such
a wonderful life here. I know it. I can feel it. Here." He
touched his hand to his heart.

He spoke so fervently it would not have been hard
to let herself be swayed. "Don't you think you're getting ahead of the game, O'Mara?" she asked reasonably. "This isn't an unequivocal no, but don't you think
we should get to know each other better before we start
talking rest-of-our-lives?"

"I know everything I need to know. Everything."

He gazed at her with a look that went deep into her
soul. She felt herself weakening. "It wouldn't always be
easy, but we could find a way to be together while I keep
on dancing. I won't be able to dance forever—just an-

other ten or twelve years," she said with a tentative laugh.

"By which time you'll be too old to have any children."

"I'm not ruling out taking off a few months to have a baby. Plenty of dancers have done it."

"Maybe they have," he said skeptically, "but what are the kids like? I don't want to raise children that way, and I'm sure you don't, either. You've already reached the top. Why not quit now? It can only be downhill from here. Besides, what's dancing compared with a family, children, building up something to pass on to them? That's what's important in life, not something that's gone as soon as you finish doing it, like a ballet."

She shrank from him, almost as if he'd physically slapped her. "If you really knew me, you never could have said what you just did." She stood up and backed away. "You don't want to marry *me*. You want to marry some idea of me. One you've made up in your head that has nothing to do with me." She watched his face harden and asked desperately, "This is a joke, isn't it?" She tried a laugh, but it echoed hollowly in the room.

"There are some things a man doesn't joke about."

"Nor a woman," she said fiercely.

She turned and ran up the stairs. In the bedroom, a single ember left from the night before glowed mockingly in the fireplace. She seized the poker and rubbed it out. *Now what do I do,* she asked herself as the poker dropped from her hand onto the hearth. She had to get out of here, but how? She found her purse where she'd dropped it beside the chair. She had some cash and credit cards in her wallet. She began to fold up her clothes, then realized she had nothing to put them in.

She glanced frantically around the room. Finally she pulled the pillows out of their cases, wrapped her fragile dress in one, placed it and the rest of her belongings in the other and slung them over her shoulder, hobo style.

How dare he, she thought with mounting fury as she fled down the stairs. While she'd been upstairs dreaming peacefully of him, he'd been wide awake plotting their future. *Their* future! Without so much as consulting her. No, he didn't need to do that—he had it all figured out.

He was pacing in the kitchen when she got downstairs. "When are you going to learn, O'Mara," she asked as she stomped past him, "that you can't throw people around as if they were footballs?"

He let her storm out of the house. She couldn't get far on foot. He'd give her a few minutes, let her settle down. He'd probably scared her. He should have eased into the subject more, not sounded so much as if he had their life all planned. Maybe she could dance for a couple more years, until he got the farm more established, until she was ready to have a baby. After all, she was only twenty-eight.

Jo stopped short a few yards from the house. She didn't have the faintest idea where she was, except that she was somewhere outside Poughkeepsie. She thought she could get a train to the city from there. Or maybe she could find a rental car outlet on the shopping strip where they'd stopped for groceries. Yes, that was a better idea. But that was a ten-minute drive away. It would take her hours to walk it. Even if she knew the way. *If I knew how to ride I'd steal a horse*, she thought. Then she remembered seeing an old bicycle propped up against the wall at the back of the barn.

Once she found it she peddled as fast as she could out to the road and turned in the direction from which they'd come the night before. It was lucky her legs were strong, for the road dipped and rose with alarming frequency. She pumped and pumped but saw neither a car to stop nor a house at which to ask directions. This place really was out in the middle of nowhere. *You'll never have to come here again,* she told herself. But the statement didn't urge her on as she'd hoped. All she could think about was what she was leaving behind.

When she first heard the noise behind her, she thought it came from an old, broken-down car. But when she turned she realized that the clip-clop was none other than horse's hooves on the asphalt roadway. O'Mara had come after her, riding tall in the saddle on Bucephalus. She peddled faster and faster, but the steady clip-clop closed in on her.

"Just where do you think you're going?" he asked easily.

"Home."

"And how do you expect to get there?"

"I'll get there."

"May I offer a suggestion?"

"Only if it's absolutely necessary."

"Let me drive you back to the city."

"Forget it. I'd rather walk."

"I didn't mean to make you angry, you know."

"I'd hate to see what could happen if you *were* trying to make me angry. You never think farther than yourself, O'Mara," she went on. She didn't want to have a conversation with him. She wanted to get as far away from him as she could, as fast as she could. She pushed harder on the creaking, squeaking pedals.

"We can work it out, Jo. Maybe you can keep dancing for a while, then when you're ready—"

"I—I can't believe you," she spluttered. "You're still making plans for me. If it's all the same to you, I'd rather run my own life. I know it's hard for a person of your temperament to grasp a simple concept like that, but—" She stopped short. Why was she wasting her breath on him when pedaling this rotten bicycle was hard enough?

"All right. You may not be ready to join me out here, but you can't tell me you didn't enjoy being with me last night. You can't tell me you weren't as moved by what happened between us as I was."

No, she couldn't deny that. "That is not the issue," she answered primly.

"Yes, it is, Jo. Think about it."

She was silent. What was the good of nights like that if the days brought wrangling and dissension? Memories, that's all a night like that produced, haunting, heart-wrenching memories.

"Won't you please let me drive you back to the city?" he asked again.

"So I can sit through two hours of hearing you plan my life for me? No, thank you." The sooner she got away from him, the better. She would put last night far behind her, put her energies into advancing her career.

"Mind if I make a suggestion, then? You do want to get to that rehearsal, don't you?"

"You know I do," she snapped.

"Turn left at the next crossroads. That'll take you out to the main road. Turn right and go to the light. Jake

Winston rents cars at his service station. I'll call him from the farm, ask him to have one ready for you and put it on my tab."

"That won't be necessary," she said stiffly. "I have several credit cards with me. I'm sure he'll honor one of them."

"It would be my pleasure," he responded sarcastically. "I brought you out here. It's my responsibility to see you get home safely."

"I'm not your responsibility, O'Mara. I'm nobody's responsibility but my own, thank you very much." She saw the crossroad ahead that he'd spoken about. It couldn't be too far to the main road now. She began to pedal for all she was worth. Her thighs were already beginning to ache from using them in this unaccustomed way. *I'm going to pay for this later*, she thought. *And not only for the bike ride.* A film of tears blurred her eyes, but she blinked it away quickly.

"I'm still going to call Jake," he insisted.

"Do whatever you want, just leave me alone." She couldn't take any more of this.

"All right, I will," he stormed angrily. He pulled on the reins, and Bucephalus turned. He dug his heels into the horse's flanks and spurred him to a gallop.

Thank heaven that was over, Jo thought as she listened to the horse's retreating hoofbeats. But it wasn't over. It would take a long time for her heart to mend, a very long time . . .

She didn't remember until she was driving toward the city that she would have to see him twice a week for several more weeks. *Oh no*, she wailed inwardly, *I can't. I won't be able to stand it.*

You'll have to. She steeled herself and tightened her grip on the steering wheel. If only she could get as tight a grip on life.

13

FOR THE FIRST TIME since he'd bought the farm, O'Mara couldn't stand being there. He wanted to leave as soon as possible—he took the stairs two at a time to gather his clothes from the bedroom. *Damn her!* he railed as his eyes fell on the crumpled bedclothes. She's ruined this place for me. *Damn her again,* he thought when he found, by the hearth, the silken cord that had bound her hair. The next time he slept in this room he would be alone, and the realization made his stomach contract in a knot.

He flew down the stairs and threw his suit into the back seat of the car. He sped to the city in record time, went straight up to his apartment and dialed Dwight Chapin. But the flunky wouldn't even consider approaching the owner about releasing O'Mara from further classes at the Metropolitan Ballet. "Don't even think about not showing up, O'Mara," Chapin warned him in polite, even dulcet tones. "That would be a breach of your contract. The legal hassles wouldn't be worth it. Believe me." O'Mara slammed down the phone and raced off to practice.

Later, after a grueling session, Rory stopped him in the locker room. "I thought you'd be smiling like the cat that got the cream today. But you're your same mean, ugly self, O'Mara. All these years Wanda's been tellin' me, 'All he needs is a good woman.' But now you've got one, it doesn't seem to be making one bit of difference. I don't know if I ought to tell Wanda. That woman hates to be wrong."

"Tell her you'll be late. I'm buying you a beer."

"Yep." Rory nodded his head. "Same ol' ugly self."

Over mugs of beer at a nearby bar, O'Mara gave Rory an abbreviated version of what had happened between him and Jo.

"I'd've walked out on you, too, man," Rory said when he'd finished.

"Thanks a lot, Washington," O'Mara growled darkly. "You're supposed to be my friend."

"I am your friend, O'Mara, but you don't know word one about dealing with women. You've got to know how to compromise. The name of the game is give-and-take. How do you think Wanda and I have made it happen all these years?"

"What about the 'magic of love'?" O'Mara asked bitterly.

"What they say about genius holds true for that magic, too, my friend. It's ninety percent perspiration, ten percent inspiration. You've got to work at it."

O'Mara harumphed and took a swig of his beer. "What I'd like to work at is getting out of those lousy ballet classes. But I called Chapin this morning, and he very cordially threatened me with legal action." He put his mug down with a thump. "I'd like to throw it all up, quit this rat race and retire to the farm."

"I wouldn't do that if I were you. You can't desert the team when we're moving in on a shot at the Super Bowl. You'd have so many broken bones you'd never ride a horse again. The guys would see to that. And the ballet classes must be doing something for us. Sure, you can say it's all the hard work and the coaching and the way we've come together as a team, but what I say is, don't mess with a good thing. But the best reason is that you'd never forgive yourself. You're not easy to know, O'Mara, but after ten years I think I've learned that much about you."

"You know I hate it when you talk sense," O'Mara said grudgingly.

Rory gave out a great laugh and clapped O'Mara on the back. "Drink up, my man. I've got a wife and children waiting on me."

JO BARELY MADE IT to the city in time to stop in at her apartment, change her clothes, get to the Metropolitan and warm up before the two-o'clock rehearsal. She accepted her colleagues' ribbing about leaving the party early and missing the company class with tight-lipped resignation. And she thanked whatever lucky stars she had left that Sasha didn't dance in the ballet that was being rehearsed, and that he wasn't there to probe more deeply into her absence.

As soon as the rehearsal ended, she went up to Mrs. Charles's office and asked to see her. After a brief wait, Mrs. Charles opened the door herself. "We're all so very proud of you, Jo," she welcomed her warmly.

"Thank you," Jo said as she stepped into the office.

"The phone hasn't stopped ringing today," Suzanne Charles added as they both sat down on the couch. "Everyone has had such glowing things to say, even more glowing than the critics, although that hardly seems possible. You've seen the reviews, of course."

"Er, not yet. I've been rather, um, busy," she said lamely.

"Yes," Mrs. Charles said with a soft smile. "You were missed at company class this morning."

Jo opened her mouth to apologize, but Mrs. Charles continued speaking. "It's all right, my dear, to miss a class now and then. I know you won't abuse the privilege. Now, then, what did you want to see me about?"

Jo's mouth went dry, but she managed to get out the difficult words. "I'd like to stop teaching the football team."

"Why, my dear, this comes as quite a surprise," Mrs. Charles remarked. "Is there a reason?"

"It's, uh, personal," Jo replied with lowered eyes.

"I see. I'm sorry, but I'm afraid it's quite impossible. We've gained so much goodwill and good publicity so far that I couldn't possibly explain a change of teacher at this late date. Neither would it be fair to the men. They've come to know and respect you, Jo. I couldn't ask them to start over now with someone new."

Jo folded her hands neatly in her lap. There was nothing she could do. Or say. She couldn't defy Mrs. Charles, and she had agreed to take on the responsibility. She would have to see it through. All she could do was try to minimize the pain she knew would accompany seeing O'Mara twice a week.

"Personal problems have a way of working themselves out, Jo," Mrs. Charles said sympathetically. "Most of them only need time."

"Thank you, Mrs. Charles," she said meekly, and rose to go.

"Take care of yourself, my dear."

I'll have to, Jo thought glumly as she let herself out of the office.

She changed to street clothes and headed slowly for her apartment, stopping along the way to fill up a plastic container at the salad bar in the Korean green grocer's on Columbus Avenue. She had two hours for eating, resting and thinking before she had to return to the theater for the evening's performance. She was only dancing in one ballet, and that part wasn't a particularly taxing one, so she could allow herself to relax and really use the time to try to sort out her very perplexing problem.

She switched the radio to her favorite classical music station and sat at her table, toying with her lettuce, trying not to let feelings of sadness or anger or hopelessness encroach upon her thoughts. During the evening rush hour the radio station mixed news and traffic reports with short pieces in a light vein. She didn't pay much attention to the radio until a medley of Sousa marches spilled rousingly from the speakers.

Not surprisingly, the music reminded her of halftime at a football game, which of course reminded her of O'Mara. But some other thought was struggling to get through, too. She pushed O'Mara aside as decisively as she had that morning, which she found a lot easier now that he wasn't following her on a horse. As soon as she had banished him, the idea beamed through.

The men knew enough steps to put them together into a ballet. She'd choreograph it to a medley of marches, set it up like a line of scrimmage, incorporate movements from the patterns and plays she'd seen in the games she'd watched. A task like that would keep her so occupied that she wouldn't have time to worry about O'Mara frowning at her from the front row. And learning a whole ballet would keep the men busy, too. O'Mara wouldn't have as much opportunity to scowl and toss barbed remarks at her.

The idea pleased her so much that she finished her salad straightaway and was able to have a restful nap before returning to the theater.

THIS MUST BE what was called psyching oneself up, Jo thought as she looked into the locker-room mirror before going off to teach her class. She checked to see that the room was empty before talking to her reflection. "You are going to go in there and treat him exactly the same as the other men, no matter how he provokes you, as he is sure to do."

She had pinned up her hair in a very severe style, and for once she regretted the Metropolitan Ballet School uniform of pink tights and a black scoop-neck leotard. She would have liked to swathe herself in a chador like an Arab woman, so that her body would be hidden from O'Mara's eyes. He was sure to take advantage of her attire—and his equally scanty clothing—with burning, taunting looks. *You can handle it*, she coached herself. She turned and marched down the hall to her classroom. What she needed was a cheerleading squad like the team had on the sidelines.

Just then she felt a hand on her shoulder. She started, then composed herself and prepared to face O'Mara. But when she whirled around she saw Rory's smiling face.

"Sorry, I didn't mean to startle you."

"That's okay. I was thinking about something else."

"Or someone else?" he suggested gently. "Well, don't you let that turkey get you down. And if he does, just remember that I'll be there rooting for you."

She smiled her thanks. "Funny, I was just thinking that I needed a cheerleader."

"I left my pom-poms home," he told her with a grin, "but I'll do my best."

"Thanks, Rory," she said as he held the door open for her. She took a deep breath and stepped in.

O'Mara was sitting on the floor near the front of the room. He studiously avoided looking at her when she came to the center of the room, and she studiously avoided looking at him when she called for attention and asked the class to go to the *barre*. She stayed away from him during the warm-up exercises and concentrated on helping the players who were standing the farthest from him. Her anger was still very close to the surface. He had ruined the most beautiful night of her life with his insensitive proposal the next morning. That, as much as the blind arrogance of the proposal itself, infuriated her.

During the exercises in the center of the floor, avoiding him was much harder. There he was, all six feet three inches of him, smack dab in her mirror view. If she took a single step backward and reached out her hand, she could touch him. But even thinking about that was foolhardy. She only had to glance at his massive shoulders, powerful chest and slim hips to want to slip into his strong arms. Despite everything, her physical reaction to him was as robust as ever. Chemistry had certain laws, and they appeared to be hard to circumvent.

When the center exercises were finished, the men began to move toward the far side of the room for the across-the-floor work that usually followed. But Jo called them back. "We'll be starting a new project today," she said. "I've begun choreographing a ballet for you. We'll learn a new sequence of it at each class until you've perfected the entire dance. You've already learned a great deal of the dance vocabulary. Now we're going to string those 'words' into sentences and paragraphs." The men were looking around at each other skeptically. "I'm sure we'll all have a lot of fun with this." Off the top of her head she added, "If it turns out as well as I think it will, maybe we can invite family and friends to a performance at the end of the season. And videotape it, too. That would give us all something to work for." The doubtful looks turned to doubtful murmurs, and Jo regretted her spontaneous suggestion. "Well, it's something to think about, at least. Why don't you all sit comfortably, and we'll listen to the music."

She played the tape, the medley of Sousa marches she had chosen the day before in the Metropolitan's music library. She could see the relief on some of the players' faces when the vigorous music began to play. She'd never have gotten them interested in the project if she'd picked something romantic or balletic, like Debussy or Tchaikovsky. By the end of the tape, several of them were moving their arms in tempo; others were tapping their feet. O'Mara sat as still as a rock. *You can't win 'em all*, she told herself stoically as she asked the men to rise.

To start off, she divided the offensive and defensive players into two groups and lined them up facing one another. She had them practice the pattern of movement—where each player would go, how and when the lines would cross—before teaching the steps they would use to effect the movements. Putting so many variables together was confusing at first. There were sharp words—for once none issued from O'Mara—when one player bumped into another. And it took more patient repetition than she had anticipated to teach the simple sequence she'd made up, but by the end of the class she had taught an eight-bar segment of the dance that the men could execute, if not perfectly, then very well.

Jo left the class feeling pleased and relieved. She and O'Mara could survive an hour and a half in each other's presence without causing a scene or tearing each other to bits. And despite the grumbling and backbiting, the men had taken wonderfully to her idea for a ballet. She had taken to it well, too. Once or twice during the class she had been so involved in what she was doing that she'd forgotten to be angry at O'Mara or to feel the hurt that throbbed with every beat of her heart.

If only she could extend the moments when she could forget or be relieved of her feelings. Then she just might make it to the end of her teaching commitment in one piece.

14

THANKSGIVING passed quickly, and Jo was then thrown into an unusually busy December. She was performing nearly every evening, and while the rehearsal schedule at the Metropolitan had diminished greatly, that only left more time for her other activities.

She had agreed to a guest appearance as the Sugar Plum Fairy in *The Nutcracker*, to be performed by the county ballet company she'd danced in as a child. She had to travel to Westchester County several times for rehearsals and spent more time than she cared to on the suburban railroad. But the trips also gave her a chance to see her family more frequently than usual.

Since her success in Sasha's ballet, she had been interviewed for newspapers, magazines—and not just dance publications—and had appeared on television and radio shows. There were scores of offers for guest appearances throughout the country and abroad to be dealt with. Plus there was *Secret Play*, as she had titled the team ballet, to be choreographed and taught to the Empire. Not to mention Christmas shopping and the unusually heavy round of holiday invitations that followed her newfound fame.

The whirlwind left her exhausted by the time she tumbled into bed at night, but no matter how tired she was, sleep was elusive. She was always aware that the other half of her bed was empty. The worst part of that was knowing exactly whom she wished was lying next to her. Of course, that was an impossible fantasy. O'Mara could get down on his hands and knees and kiss her callused feet, but there was no way she was giving up her career. She might as well cut off one of her arms.

Not that she had any indication that O'Mara was willing to kiss so much as her hand, much less her feet. During the past couple of classes, after a long, stony silence, they had begun to exchange a civil word or two, but neither of them had made any attempt at reconciliation. Since it had taken that long for them to get to the speaking stage, there seemed little hope for a true reconciliation in the very little time she had left with the Empire.

Unless something disastrous happened, the team would probably clinch their division title and make it to the league play-offs. But it wasn't at all certain that they could beat the other division title holders. If the Empire lost to that stiff competition, her job would be over; if the team won the league title, classes would continue until the Super Bowl in mid-January. But even if the Empire—as impossible as it had seemed at the beginning of the season—did play in the Super Bowl, she had only a few more chances to see O'Mara. After Super Sunday, at the latest, he would be gone from her life.

But not from her memory. No, never from her memory. She knew she would never again feel about anyone the way she did about O'Mara. Which made it all the more frustrating and heartbreaking that there was nothing to be done about the situation. He couldn't give her what she wanted, and she couldn't give him what he wanted. It was as simple as that.

After the season she wouldn't even be able to watch him on TV. She watched every Empire game she could, and she had splurged on a new color set and a video recorder to tape the games she had to miss. All she would have left of him would be a few glimpses on cold, hard videotape. Still, her need to see him, if only that way, sent her to the TV for the meager comfort of watching films on cassette when she couldn't sleep at night. And meager comfort, she had learned, was better than none at all.

She pushed the class hard to learn the whole of *Secret Play* before the end of regular season play. It meant a lot to her to see it completed, to see the evidence of having taken a roomful of growling gorillas and tamed them into men who could learn and dance a ballet. Once again she had broached the subject of having the finished product videotaped, but the response from the players had been lukewarm, to say the least. She had time to work on them, though, to bring them around. That wouldn't be as hard a job as it once had been. She had grown fond of the team over the months and they of her, and she thought she'd win out in the end, even if it took some sweet-talking and feather smoothing.

For the class before Christmas, Jo prepared a modest gift for each of the men. She bought small Christmas stockings in the dime store, wrote the men's names on them with glue and glitter and filled each one with little presents—candy canes, foil-wrapped chocolate Santas, football-shaped key rings, football trading cards, and molded plastic statuettes representing characters from Steven Spielberg's film, *The Empire Strikes Back*. She made sure that O'Mara got one of Darth Vader, and hoped he'd have a sense of humor about it.

On the morning of that pre-Christmas class, Jo
stowed her box of presents in the corner behind the
piano and went back to the change room for a few
minutes. She had made it a practice not to arrive at class
until it was time to teach and to leave immediately after the bows. While she was working she could control
her feelings about O'Mara, but she was afraid that any
unoccupied time spent in the room with him would
leave her vulnerable.

At one minute to ten, she entered the room and
greeted her class. "Great game Sunday, fellas," she
complimented them. With that win the Empire had
clinched a berth in the league play-offs. "It's lookin'
good for the Super Bowl." The team showed its spirit
with a few impromptu cheers and a round of hand
clapping. She waited for the men to settle down and
started right in on the class.

"Good morning," O'Mara said as he passed her on
the way to the *barre*.

"Good morning," she replied somewhat stiffly. She
still felt wary around him. He hadn't erupted yet, but
she knew how little it took to set him off. Then he
smiled at her. Just a simple smile, not a smirk, nothing
sardonic. *Maybe the Christmas spirit is getting to him*,
she thought. In light of the season she smiled back, a
bit tentatively, but with warmth and, she realized as the
edges of her mouth curled up, genuine pleasure. It was
awfully nice to be smiled at and smile back. Awfully
nice. *Oh, no, you don't*, she told herself sternly, *that's
hope you're feeling. It was only a smile, don't go making a song and a dance about it.* But the smiles kept
coming throughout the class.

She taught the final eight-bar sequence of *Secret Play* that morning, and the men danced the ballet from start to finish for the first time. There were plenty of mistakes but no major calamities. When the music ended the team stood uncertainly in their final poses, but Jo could have jumped for joy. "You did it! That was terrific." The men started to smile and punch at one another playfully.

"Hey, we did it!" Rory crowed. "Let's hear it for us." A cheer rang out through the room.

"And for Jo," O'Mara added.

His eyes caught hers and held them firmly. A louder cheer rocked the room, but Jo hardly heard it. She was trying to read the silent communication he was sending to her. But before she could break the code, she broke the gaze. *There's no use starting up again with him*, she lectured herself. It could only mean more heartbreak, worse heartbreak.

"Thank you, thank you," she said to the men. "But let's not get carried away with ourselves. That was terrific, but far from perfect." A groan rippled through the room. She pointed out the mistakes she'd noted. "We've got time to do it once more. Any questions?"

She answered a couple as she rewound the tape, then called for places. The men did themselves proud. They had heeded her criticisms and so greatly improved their execution of the dance. She was also able to step back and take a critical look at her own choreography. She had done herself proud, too, she decided. Though the movements were simple, they were well arranged; the interplay between the two lines was varied and interesting. Not too bad for a first work.

She gave the men a few pointers to remember for the next class and led them in the final bows. She had planned to distribute her presents to the men as they left the room; she started for the corner to retrieve them. She heard Rory call her name and turned to him.

"Don't hurry off, please. We, um, well, we all chipped in and got you a little something for Christmas." The player nearest the door stepped outside and returned with a pair of boxes, which he handed to her. Rory continued. "We know we've been rough on you at times, but we all wanted you to know that we've come to think of you as 'one of the guys.'"

"Thank you," she said, deeply touched. "I don't know what to say, except that I've enjoyed teaching you and that I've learned a lot. And not only about teaching dance. For the first time in my life, I know what a lateral pass is."

"Awwright!" a player shouted. "Let's hear it for Jo." A chorus of cheers and applause rose up.

Jo held up her hands and yelled above the noise, "Cut it out, you guys, you're making me blush!"

"Aren't you going to open your present?" Rory asked.

"You didn't give me a chance yet." She untied the ribbon and slipped the paper off the larger of the two boxes. Beneath the lid she found two small but exquisite woodcuts of traditional Japanese dancers, nestled side by side in a soft bed of white tissue paper. "They're lovely," she said quietly. "Absolutely lovely. Thank you so much. I'll think of you all every time I look at them." She felt a lump forming in her throat as she slipped the paper off the second box. It was from her favorite *chocolatier*. She lifted the lid and found row after row of sugar-dusted truffles. "Trying to make me fat, eh?"

she blustered. It was that or break down and cry in front of them all. She thought she knew from the chocolates who was responsible for choosing the presents.

"Blame O'Mara," Rory said, confirming her suspicion. "He's the one who picked the presents."

"Thank you," she said to O'Mara, and bit the inside of her lip to stem her tears. "You chose well." He nodded and lowered his eyes, apparently as affected by the moment as she was. "I have something for all of you, too," she said brightly, and hurried to the corner to get her box. She set herself up by the door, handed each man his stocking and thanked each one personally for her presents.

O'Mara hung back so that he was the last to leave the room. "I'm glad you liked the presents, Jo. Merry Christmas."

"Merry Christmas to you, too."

There was a long, awkward pause. "Are you doing anything special for Christmas?" he asked.

"I'll be spending the day with my family, as usual. And you?"

"My brother and his family and my mother are coming down to the farm. They've never been there. I usually go upstate, but with the play-offs this year I won't be able to make it."

"That's nice for you. I'm sure they'll enjoy it, too." Talking to him was so difficult. There was so much left unsaid, so much that couldn't be said. Part of her wanted to rip down the barricades between them, but she chose to stay safely behind them. The common ground they might meet on could well be made of quicksand.

O'Mara shifted uneasily, made a move to go and aborted it. "We have one more class with you before the play-offs, right?"

"Right."

"I guess I'll see you then," he said haltingly. "Merry Christmas," he wished her once more.

"The presents are perfect. Really they are."

"Good. I wanted to give you something that would make you think of me. Once in a while." He rested a finger on her cheek for the briefest of moments.

"I will," she whispered hoarsely. He left the room, and the door closed softly behind him.

That was it, she thought. *That was our goodbye. It's all over now.* She walked over to the opened boxes and looked down at the woodcuts. They were so very beautiful, so much to her taste. Only someone who knew her very well could have chosen them.

She knelt down to examine the prints and nibbled a truffle as she pored over them. The candy was sweet and delicious, but for once it didn't make her feel any better.

IT HAD BEEN WORTH IT, O'Mara told himself as he left the Metropolitan's building, just to see her delight when she'd opened the presents. He had tried to weasel out of the job, hadn't wanted to put himself through the pain of shopping for something that would please her. But the team, led by Rory, had insisted. Rory had told him a hundred times in a hundred different ways that he was being a fool where Jo was concerned, but O'Mara couldn't face up to reopening the still-fresh wounds. Yet he had enjoyed the shopping, and when he'd seen how much she'd liked the presents, the hard knot inside had begun to soften.

He decided to walk in Central Park for a while before getting his car and reporting to practice. As he walked he kept thinking about what Rory had said to him about compromise, about having to work at love the same way you worked at anything you cared about. He did care for Jo, cared so deeply for her that he couldn't imagine his life without her. But if he didn't do something about it quickly, she would be gone.

But what could he do? He needed someone who could share his life on the farm, be at his side, at least part of the time. And she needed to dance. Maybe if they could both give up something, they could figure out a way to be together. And they were meant to be together. Every time he thought about their night at the farmhouse he knew that.

"There has to be a way. There has to be," he repeated to himself over and over. Out of the mantra came an answer: *Yes, but you're never going to find it on your own.*

15

ON THE SUNDAY between Christmas and the New Year, Jo curled up in front of the TV, her box of truffles in her lap, to watch the Empire in the playoffs. Sasha had invited the company to his place for a play-off party, but she had begged off. She'd been riding an emotional pogo stick for days; her feelings had been up and down and all over the place. She needed some time alone to help them settle down.

She paid more attention to the chocolate she was nibbling than to the commentators' predictions for the game, but when Patti Pringle appeared on screen and announced a prerecorded interview with the Empire quarterback, she glued her eyes to the set. Pringle and O'Mara started with a few minutes' banter about strategy, but then Pringle asked a question that set Jo's pulse racing. "How much do you think your ballet training has contributed to your winning season?"

"Of course it's hard to separate all the factors," O'Mara answered. "Naturally our coaches deserve the bulk of the credit, but the ballet training has given us a shared experience off the playing field. It's done a lot to galvanize the team, besides teaching us different ways of moving and improving the connection between our brains and our feet. We owe a vote of thanks to our teacher at the Metropolitan Ballet, Jo Sherbourne."

He smiled into the camera, in such a way that Jo felt he was smiling only for her. *Stop being so silly*, she told herself. *He knows the value of charming the public as well as anyone on the planet. However*, she thought with a certain satisfaction, *there's no reason for him to mention me specifically.*

"If you go on to the Super Bowl—" Pringle began her next question.

"When we go on," O'Mara interrupted.

"If or when," she conceded, "do you think the Empire's owner will come out of hiding?"

"I should hope the man would come forward to accept the credit he's due. But if he still wants to retain his anonymity, that's up to him."

Jo sat up straight at that answer, and even a seasoned pro like Patti Pringle couldn't hide her surprise. "That's quite a different stance than you were taking at the beginning of the season."

"Yes," O'Mara allowed.

"Can you tell me what's caused this change of heart?"

He launched another smile into the camera, and again Jo felt it traveling straight to her like a well-programmed rocket ship. "Let's just say that I'm cultivating a more mellow approach to life these days."

"Except on the field," Pringle prompted.

"A little mellowness goes a long way," he replied.

The camera cut to a close-up of Patti Pringle. "We'll see the kind of yardage that mellow approach racks up later today, viewers. I also talked to the Panthers' QB this morning, and here's what he had to say."

Jo didn't hear a word the opposing quarterback had to say. She was too astounded by O'Mara's interview. He sounded like a changed man. He was still charming and dangerously handsome, but where were the bluster and bravado? Any mention of the owner usually made him come out of the corner swinging, and yet he hadn't put his dukes up once. It was too bad he hadn't been more like that before, when they. . . She stemmed the thought. It was over, she reminded herself. They had played their goodbye scene at the class before Christmas. She reached for another truffle and concentrated on the pregame show taking place on the field.

By the end of the final quarter, Jo had a distinctly rum tummy, as much from the tension of the game as from overindulgence in chocolate truffles. One thing about the Empire, they never won big; they eked out their victories, foot by foot and in the last seconds of the game. They had done it again in the play-offs.

The previous three hours had been among the most nerve-racking she had ever spent. After all, she had more riding on the game than dedicated fans or those who had bet on the outcome. Whether the Empire won or lost determined if she would see, ever again, the man she had given herself to, heart and body.

She told herself all afternoon that it would be better if the Empire lost, if she didn't have to see O'Mara again. But she wasn't ready for that yet, no matter how many times she told herself it was over between them. Yet it wasn't only O'Mara who had her rooting for the team. Over the season she had developed tremendous loyalty to all the men. She knew how much it meant to the players to win, and she wanted to see them do it.

And they did. On a brilliant fake from the twenty-yard line, O'Mara circumvented the Panther defense and scored six points, to put the Empire ahead 23-20 with four seconds on the clock. Their punter missed the final kick, but the time was used up nevertheless. The team that had long been known as the Keystone Kops of football was on its way to the Super Bowl.

THE PLAYERS WERE IN an ebullient mood on Tuesday morning, as well they should have been. Their pride and pocketbooks had swelled over the weekend, and further fame and fortune glittered on the horizon. Jo felt rather ebullient herself; she joked and kidded with the players almost as if she were Patti Pringle. Their presents had truly made her feel she was "one of the guys."

O'Mara joined in the good-natured ribbing, and her spirits rose as they had during the preplay-off interview. She let them. There would be time enough after the class, after the Super Bowl, for letting the air out of the balloon that was lifting her feet off the ground.

The men were especially enthusiastic about rehearsing the ballet. They danced it once through, after which Jo noted the weak spots. Then they began to polish their performance. "We've got two groups here. Neither of you are aware enough of what the other's doing. That's why you're bumping into each other so much and missing so many steps. Offense, sit down at the front of the room. I want you to learn what the defensive line is doing."

She had the defense dancers demonstrate their part three times. Then she surprised everyone by asking the offense to get up and duplicate what they had just seen. "We can't do that," O'Mara protested.

"Yes, you can. All you have to do is concentrate. Remember what you've seen first and then tell your body to do it. You've got five minutes to talk among yourselves and reconstruct the movements. And no coaching from the other side," she ordered.

They didn't do half badly. O'Mara and Rory both had good eyes, and the men were surprised by how much they could remember and do without rehearsal. "See how far you've come," she congratulated them.

"And we didn't even know it," O'Mara answered. "There's a lesson in that," he said in a neutral tone but with his eyes aimed directly at Jo. Her balloon seemed to hit an updraft, and she rose with it. *What if,* she said to herself, *what if that wasn't goodbye last week? What if that was hello in a language I didn't understand?*

After the defense had learned the offense's part, they put *Secret Play* back together again. The difference was immediately apparent to teacher and players. "Good work," Jo called to them. "The next big step is to stop thinking about the steps. Trust that you know them and *dance!*"

There was a collision or two caused by the enthusiasm with which the team took up her challenge, but for the first time she felt that the men understood what it meant to dance, that the point was not only to do the steps correctly but to let a spirit shine through them.

"Maybe we should get this videotaped," Rory suggested after the next run-through. "We could invite Pringle. It sure would be some unusual pre-Super Bowl publicity."

"There's enough hype going down already," O'Mara griped.

"You're just sore because you're afraid the owner's gonna steal your thunder," Rory countered.

"Who do you think it's going to turn out to be, Jo?" one of the men asked.

"I haven't the faintest idea. But you've got to win, or none of us will know," she reminded them.

After the Empire had won the league title, Dwight Chapin's office had issued a press release to announce that the team's owner would make himself known after the Super Bowl game—but only if the Empire won. It had been front-page news, along with the results of the game, in every newspaper in the country. Every television and radio station had carried the news, too. The nation hadn't indulged in such rife speculation since everyone had tried to figure out who had shot J. R. Ewing.

"We'll win, all right," O'Mara declared.

"We'd better, if we know what's good for us," someone shot back. "If O'Mara doesn't find out who the owner is, he'll be eatin' us raw for supper after the game."

"Yeah, you put on a good act for the television audience," one of the linebackers put in. "But you can't fool us. We know you better than that, O'Mara."

O'Mara shrugged off the comment. "Think what you want, but I really don't care anymore. Some guy wants to make grandstand plays, let him. Let's cut the chatter now, we're wasting Jo's time." He looked deeply into her eyes again.

"Not my time, our time," she said. Though she hadn't planned her answer that way, once again the words they had spoken had a personal as well as a public meaning. She turned away swiftly to go to the tape recorder. "Once more please, gentlemen, before the final bows."

After class O'Mara approached her. "I was wondering if you had time for lunch. I, um, I think we should talk."

"Is there anything to talk about?" she asked warily.

"I think so."

"I'll meet you in the hall after I've changed," she said, and hurried from the room. She was flushed and warm by the time she reached the locker room. She doused her face with cold water and let water from the cold tap run over her wrists to slow her surging blood. It was so hard not to be excited, even though she knew that what he had to say to her might be painful. Her fingers fumbled with buttons and zippers as she put on the sweater and slacks she'd worn that morning and bundled herself up in her down coat.

O'Mara was waiting in the hall when she emerged, his hands thrust into the pockets of his leather bombardier's jacket, the heels of his cowboy boots clicking nervously against the tiles. They stood facing each other for a moment, both smiling as awkwardly as teenagers on a blind date.

"Where would you like to go?" he asked.

"I . . ." She hesitated. "I know a great hot dog stand in Central Park." Being outdoors, walking, the scenery constantly changing, was more appealing that sitting in a crowded, overheated restaurant. "Unless you think it's too cold," she added anxiously.

"No, no," he assured her. "I could use the fresh air."

The sun was shining brightly on Broadway, but it brought little warmth to the bracing air. They crossed the wide avenue quickly and headed for the park.

"So what have you been doing?" O'Mara sounded like someone making conversation with an acquaintance he'd unexpectedly encountered.

"Keeping busy," she answered in the same impersonal tone.

"I noticed," he told her. "For a few weeks there I saw you practically every time I opened a newspaper or magazine or turned on the TV."

She had made something of a splash in the media after the debut of Sasha's ballet, it was true. And she was flattered and pleased that he'd been following her success.

They entered the park, and a gust of wind swept down on them. He pulled up the fur collar of his jacket. "I haven't had much else to do besides playing football and looking after the farm," he said significantly.

She steered them to a path beside the Sheep Meadow. "Isn't that enough to keep you busy?"

"Not really. It left me a lot of time for thinking." When she didn't reply he added, "About you, about us."

Jo stuffed her mittened hands farther into the pockets of her coat. Though she was dressed very warmly, she still shivered at his words. "Come to any conclusions?" she asked as lightly as she could.

"That's the trouble with thinking. Real thinking, that is. It raises more questions than answers." Suddenly he began to laugh and point ahead of him. The path they were on gave a good view of the white stone bank shell, where in summer a variety of concerts were held, everything from opera to ethnic folk music. On the stage, sheltered under the arching canopy, was a silver cart, its yellow umbrella a flag celebrating the operator's ingenious way to beat the cold. "Is that your four-star hot dog vendor?"

"Unless there's a show scheduled," she said with a merry laugh, "and he's the curtain raiser."

As they drew nearer, they first heard the strains of a symphony orchestra and then saw the large portable cassette player at the edge of the stage. "He isn't the curtain raiser, he's the whole show," O'Mara commented.

"Perfect music for a picnic," Jo said, recognizing the piece. "Beethoven's Sixth, the *Pastorale*," she said in response to his questioning look.

The vendor, a small man made large by the many layers of clothes he wore, stood up from his camp stool when they arrived at the foot of the stage. He made no attempt to turn down the music, which was quite loud at close range, and Jo shouted a question about hot drinks. "Coffee, tea or hot chocolate," he offered, pointing to the two-burner propane hot plate he had rigged up on the cart. A kettle of hot water simmered on one, a covered pot on the other. "Tomato soup, too. From a can, I'm afraid, but I doctor it up real good."

Jo and O'Mara both asked to try the vendor's soup, which was not only warming but deliciously spicy. She asked what he'd put in the soup, but he winked at her and said it was a trade secret. They ordered hot dogs and then walked down the mall beside the band shell to enjoy their feast at one of the many empty benches beneath the bare trees. The music floated to them in snatches, depending on the drift of the wind.

"Best restaurant in town," O'Mara said as they sat down. "No crowds, no waiting, good food, good music." He paused and looked deeply into her eyes. "And good company."

She couldn't have felt any warmer if she'd been on a sunny beach in the Caribbean. "Don't ever say I don't take you to great places," she said brightly.

"You've taken me to some of the best places I've ever been."

"Have I?"

"Places of the heart, Jo, the soul."

They ate silently for several moments, digesting the weighty words and feelings that accompanied their light meal. *He's making such an effort to open up*, Jo thought, realizing how hard she had tried in past weeks to close herself off. She'd never have been brave enough to approach him the way he was approaching her. "What are those questions you mentioned before," she asked, "the ones you've been thinking about?"

"It's one question that has me the most stymied: what are we doing apart?"

She answered with the question that had been bothering her for so long. "It's the flip side of the one I've been mostly avoiding: how can we be together?"

"We can work at it. We can try."

"But we want such completely different things."

"Do we? Think about it, Jo."

"What do you mean?" she asked cautiously.

He began to pile up their used cups and napkins. "Let's walk. I'm getting cold." He stood and lobbed the trash neatly into the nearest refuse container. He held out his hand to her, and she hesitated before putting hers into it. He helped her up from the bench, and they started down the mall, both self-consciously aware of the feel of the other's touch, muffled though it was by her woolen mittens and his leather gloves.

"While I've been doing all this thinking I've been making one assumption. That you weren't faking your feelings that night in the farmhouse."

"I wasn't," she said quietly. "But that was one night. We can't make a life out of that."

"And we can't go back to before it happened. I can't, that is," he said, remembering to speak only for himself and not for her. "The only way to go is forward."

She had been living in limbo since that night, too. "But to where?" she asked.

"To a life we can both accept, both be happy with."

"Such as?"

"I don't have to retire this year, I can keep playing, get more help at the farm to keep it growing. Then I can spend more time in the city with you during the Metropolitan's season. You can cut down on your commitments outside the season. We can build you a studio at the house. If we both want to, we can work it out."

"What about your dreams?" He was coming very close to convincing her. But it all came back to dreams—his dreams, the strength of them, the way they clashed with hers. They were the cause of the trouble, and they had a habit of sticking around.

"Those are just dreams, Jo. You're reality."

THOSE WORDS WERE A THEME that played almost constantly in her head as the Super Bowl approached. No matter what she did—danced, taught, walked, talked—they were always in the background, and often in the foreground. She composed a thousand variations on the theme, some jagged and jarring, some sad and haunting, others lyrical and romantic. Sometimes they all played at the same time, and she thought she would go mad from the din. At other times, though, the possibilities blended into a beautiful symphony, and she wanted to capture their harmony forever.

But all the music in her head brought her no closer to a decision about O'Mara, about them. He had put the ball in play; now it was up to her to carry it. And she didn't know which way to go. So she ran in place until she was more weary than she had ever been.

16

JO WAS AWAKE to see Super Sunday dawn clear and cold. She huddled under the covers listening to the radio until at last it was a halfway reasonable time to to get up. She had decided to skip class this once. There was no way she could have dragged herself through that grueling hour and a half and then gone to the game.

The Super Bowl was to be played in Empire Stadium and, along with Mrs. Charles, she had received via Dwight Chapin an invitation to watch it from the owner's box. Brunch was to be served before the kick-off, and Mrs. Charles had arranged for her driver to arrive at Jo's at eleven o'clock.

She cleared herself a space in the living room, gave herself a short *barre* holding on to the back of a chair, stretched on the floor for a while and then went in to take a bath. She dawdled in the tub, took extra time with her hair, her makeup, brushed every speck of lint off her black velvet trousers—twice—tried on every sweater she owned before settling on the powder-blue cashmere with the cowl collar. Even then it was only ten forty-five.

She was jittery on every count she could think of. If the team didn't win they'd be terribly disappointed; if O'Mara didn't lead them to victory, he'd never find out who the owner was. She was rather curious to know who he was herself. After all, he was the person who'd brought her and O'Mara together. He'd ordered the ballet classes, arranged dinner that night for her and O'Mara in his box, had been the cause of their first row.

Would he now be the one who brought them together for their last meeting? She'd been thinking about everything O'Mara had said to her in the park. He had made no further attempts to approach her, and she hadn't gone to him. They seemed to have made a tacit bargain to give each other space and time to think through their situation. In the last classes they had been more at ease with each other than at any time recently, but still they had both held on to a certain reserve. Despite all her thinking, she didn't know what to do. O'Mara did seem to have been changed by their experience. His hot head had cooled considerably; arrogance had bowed to a more controlled self-assurance. But was that enough?

And herself? Her feelings were not in doubt—she felt as strongly about him as she had on their one perfect night. It was the consequences of her feelings that still worried her. How much was she willing to give up to be with him? She wanted to know, needed to know but was reluctant to find out. Her life had been dance, dance, dance for as long as she could remember. Would he break up that symmetry—or add a new dimension?

The sound of her doorbell snapped her out of her thoughts. She glanced out the window and saw Mrs. Charles's car double-parked in front of her building. She threw on her coat and left the apartment.

"You look lovely, my dear," Mrs. Charles said when she sat down beside the older woman in the back seat.

"Oh, thank you," she answered, surprised by the compliment. She had fussed over herself so long she was unsure of the result.

"It must be all the excitement that's brought such a bloom to your cheeks."

"I've never been to a Super Bowl game before," Jo said, begging the real question of her flushed cheeks.

"I've been to several with Oliver. They certainly do get the blood moving."

When Mrs. Charles mentioned her late husband Jo felt a sudden sinking in the stomach, an insight into what it would be like to lose the man you had loved and lived with. The weeks without O'Mara had been bad enough. What if you knew your man was never coming back? "I'm sorry Mr. Charles isn't here today. He would have enjoyed this."

"He certainly would have," Suzanne Charles agreed. She patted Jo's gloved hand with hers. "I've made my peace, my dear. There's great comfort in that."

Yes, Jo thought knowingly. If only she could come to her own kind of peace about O'Mara. There would be great comfort in that.

Godfrey the butler, dressed in his formal morning suit, greeted them at the door of the owner's box. He helped Mrs. Charles off with her mink and took Jo's more modest wool coat. There were several people in the room, Dwight Chapin among them, and he introduced Jo and Mrs. Charles to the head coach's wife and children, to his personal assistant and her husband, to the team's administrative executives and their families. A bartender was on hand, and the caterers were putting the finishing touches on a lavish buffet. As Jo had suspected, the owner himself was nowhere in sight.

The company ate and chatted until Godfrey summoned them to their seats for the gala pregame show. The delicious food and drink had served to dull her nerves for a while, but as the first band struck up and marched onto the field, a new round of nerves and excitement gripped her.

When the game started and Jo heard O'Mara's voice come over the loudspeaker in the box, reeling off signals, she nearly jumped out of her chair. The owner had had the microphone that relayed quarterback's signals to the coaches on the sidelines connected to his private box, as well. Once Jo got used to hearing O'Mara's voice, she felt that she had a special link to him and the team, and she imagined her good-luck thoughts finding their way down through the speaker onto the field. She knew that was silly, but it made her feel she was doing something to support the team's efforts.

Early on, the game established itself as a running and passing game, not one where the teams slugged it out on the line of scrimmage. Jo used her newly discovered telepathic "hot line" to the team constantly, but not entirely successfully. When the halftime whistle blew, the St. Louis Leopards were ahead by two points.

She sank into her chair as a bank struck up and a precision dance team strutted onto the field. "Whew!" she exclaimed to Mrs. Charles. "This is a real nail-biter."

"Isn't it?" Suzanne Charles responded with enviable calm.

Coffee and dessert were served; Jo took a large piece of coconut layer cake to help while away the long interval. There was as much talk in the room about meeting "the boss" as there was about the game. She joined in, but her spirit was down in the locker room with the team, urging them on to victory. The team's winning was the only thing she allowed herself to think about. Thinking about her personal dilemma with O'Mara had led her in so many circles that she didn't think she could stand being any dizzier. The effort of avoiding another tailspin was taxing, and she was relieved when Godfrey once again summoned the group to the box.

The Empire took the field with vigor and, to the delight of everyone in the box and the fans in the stadium, they scored a touchdown in the first minutes of the third quarter. They held the lead well into the fourth quarter, until it looked as though the Leopards intercepted a pass O'Mara had sent to Rory and in two decisive plays had moved back into the lead.

With only one minute and seconds on the clock, when it seemed that all was lost, the Empire managed to regain possession of the ball. The crowd rose to their feet in a single movement, and stayed standing through the final tense minute of play. The team's first two attempts to make a first down were unsuccessful; the Leopard line seemed impregnable. Soon the time on the clock was whittled down to forty-five seconds.

O'Mara called time and held his men in the next huddle for as long as he could. Finally they reassembled on the field, and his voice boomed over the loudspeaker. "Set! Hut! *Secret Play!*" The Empire swung into action.

"What are they doing?" Mrs. Charles clutched Jo's arm. "It looks like a ballet."

"It is!" Jo exclaimed with amazement. "It's the ballet I choreographed." She sprang up out of her seat, jumping up and down, waving her hands over her head. But

214 No Passing Fancy

she wasn't rooting. She was calling out the steps of the dance.

The Leopard defense was in absolute disarray. They didn't know where the ball was, didn't know how to cover their assigned players. The Leopards kept looking to the sidelines for help from their coaches, but the coaches were all yelling different instruction, adding to the pandemonium.

The Empire kept the dance going long enough to run the clock down to the last crucial second. Then the ball was passed to O'Mara, and before the other team noticed, he was steaming toward the goal line. He was at the twenty-yard line before the Leopards started to give chase. By then it was too late. Just as the clock ran out, O'Mara ran between the posts and dashed the ball down in the end zone. The referee's arms went up, and the figures on the scoreboard changed.

The stadium went wild. They were all on their feet cheering and screaming, waving pennants, hats, small children—whatever was at hand. The scene in the owner's box was not much different. Dwight Chapin whirled the head coach's three-year-old daughter around in a circle; the administrators were whooping and stomping like the Apache after defeating Custer; even Godfrey was applauding and wearing an expression that could easily be taken for a smile.

The only two people in the stadium who weren't contributing to the bedlam were Jo and Mrs. Charles. Jo sat stock-still in her seat, unable to believe she hadn't imagined what had just happened. Mrs. Charles hovered over her, asking if she wanted a glass of water or an aspirin.

Down on the field the Empire were running riot, jumping jubilantly, slapping one another on the back or the rump, hugging each other in a great clump. From the center of the mass of bodies, a single one rose. O'Mara was hoisted onto the shoulders of his teammates. They carried him to the fifty-yard line and stood right under the owner's box. "Jo! Jo! Jo!" they chanted. A horde of photographers, camera operators and reporters surrounded them.

It took Jo a moment to realize they were calling for her. With Mrs. Charles's help, she pulled herself up and went to the front of the box. Godfrey opened the sliding Plexiglas panels, and she stepped out onto the small balcony that overlooked the field. There was so much energy on the field and in the stadium and her body was generating so much heat that she didn't feel the sharp cold at all.

She looked out from the balcony and, despite all the people, all the action, all the noise, all the distractions, her eyes met O'Mara's straightaway. They beckoned her, called to her, enticed her until they moved her physically, and she leaned out over the rails toward him.

Still fixing his eyes on her, he leaned down and said something to the team. After a few seconds of uncertain activity, O'Mara was hoisted to a standing position on the shoulders of two of the team's toughest tackles. They walked him to within arm's reach of the balcony. He held out his arms to her. "Come out here where you belong!" he yelled.

She looked at him incredulously, then heard the team begin to chant her name again. He wanted her; they wanted her. In an instant the decision she had been agonizing over was made. She had to go to him; they were meant to be together. She knew it now for the truth, so certainly that she wondered how the doubts had arisen.

She perched on the balcony railing and flung her legs over the side. Gaining purchase on the bottom rung, she threw herself into O'Mara's arms, trusting he would catch her as easily as Sasha did during a performance. His strong arms closed around her, and soon they were both balanced on the team's shoulders like a team of bare-back riders in the circus. Someone tossed up a team blanket, and they draped it around their shoulders.

"The time has come!" O'Mara yelled as soon as Jo was safely settled. "We won the game. Send out the Emperor. Now!"

The team picked up a new chant. "Now! Now! Now!" Soon every voice in the stadium had joined the chorus.

Dwight Chapin stepped out onto the balcony and steadied himself on the railing. He looked like a man who had just pulled his finger from a live electric socket. Shakily he raised a single hand and called for quiet. Eventually the noise dampened to a dull roar. "I, er, I . . ." He fumbled for words. He wiped his forehead with the back of his hand and looked out at the crowd.

"Now! Now! Now!!" the chant rose up again.

Chapin composed himself and asked for quiet once more. "The owner is here, ladies and gentlemen." He said it three or four times before everyone realized the moment had, indeed, come. An expectant hush fell over the stadium. He retreated into the owner's box.

Suzanne Charles stepped on to the balcony, and there was a long moment of dead silence. Jaws gaped and eyes bulged all over the stadium. Thousands of people breathed in as one. Then all hell broke loose.

Jo and O'Mara turned to one another. The team wobbled beneath them, and she clutched at his shoulders to stay upright. His face was black with fury, but when he took in the absolute shock on hers, he threw back his head and began to laugh uncontrollably.

"The joke is sure on me," he said to her when he got ahold of himself.

"And on me," Jo said, still in a state of shock. "I can't believe it. How could she have fooled us all? I don't believe it."

They held on to each other for more than dear life as the team, caught up in their own disbelief and merriment, jiggled and jolted beneath them.

Above them, Suzanne Charles waited with her usual equanimity for the right moment to speak. When it came her voice was clear and forceful. "I once bet my late husband, Oliver—who was a great fan of the Empire—that if I had the team in my ballet school for three months they'd be unbeatable." She paused and looked heavenward. "Oliver, wherever you are, and I hope you're listening, *I was right!*" For just a moment she lost her cool detachment and, clasping her hands over her head like a prizefighter accepting a decision, waved them jubilantly.

Pandemonium reigned once again, but O'Mara managed to attract the team's attention long enough to get them to put him and Jo down on the ground. He maneuvered her out of the worst of the chaos and held her close in their own charmed circle.

"If ballet and football can merge and win out like they just did," he shouted over the noise, "don't you think we can solve our few piffling problems?"

They *would* find a way, she repeated to herself, just as O'Mara had found a way to beat the Leopards. They had a foundation to build on. All they had to do now was proceed with courage and creativity. His grandstand play had taught her that. "We can if we want to," she answered.

"And do we want to?"

"We want to!" The answer came from the deepest part of her, because she was free from the fears and the equivocation that had helped keep them apart for too long.

He gazed at her lovingly for a long while and then brought his lips to hers for an endlessly ardent kiss. "I've loved you too long from afar, Jo," he said when he finally released her. "I've known ever since that night at the farm that I could never stop loving you."

"I love your bravery," she said. "Only a very brave man would have taken me for that walk in the park that day. Only a very brave man would have held out his arms to me in front of all those millions of people. You weren't afraid of the humiliation if I refused. I want to be as brave as you are and trust that I can be with you without losing myself."

"If you lost yourself, Jo my love, there wouldn't be any us." His mouth covered hers again, and she was floating free on a sea of rapture. "I know we may be apart for longer than I like sometimes."

"And I may have to refuse engagements I'd really love to take."

"But we'll be together," they said in unison.

"I'll keep you warm and safe, Jo."

"And I'll always be there for you, O'Mara. Always."

He crushed her to him and said, "I thought I'd never hear you say that to me."

"I'll say that to you for the rest of our lives. However," she said with a twinkle in her eyes, "I feel it's only fair to warn you that if you get out of line I will have no compunction about calling you—"

He clapped a hand over her mouth. "Don't say it," he warned.

She vigorously nodded her assent, and he took his hand away. "I'll call you Twinkle Toes," she blurted out as soon as her mouth was free.

His face darkened for a stormy second, and then he burst out laughing. "That's one moniker I won't mind, my love. Because it will always remind me of how we met. As if I could ever forget." He put his arm around her waist and began to lead her off the field. "Come on, let's get out of this loony bin and go someplace quiet."

They hadn't taken three steps when they were stopped by Patti Pringle's microphone. "Not so fast, you two. You're not leaving without giving me the whole scoop. From the looks on your faces and the way you're sneaking away, it must be something very big."

O'Mara grinned at her and pushed the mike away. "I'll make you a deal, Pringle. I won't tell anyone how wrong you almost were about Barton Harley, and you won't tell anyone about Jo and me." The reporter's mouth opened for an angry retort, but his next words closed it again. "Until we're ready."

"When we are, Patti, you'll be the first to know," Jo assured her.

"I just want to know, O'Mara," Patti said, nodding in Jo's direction, "who told you so?" She embraced them both in her large, long arms. "Off the record, I'm very happy for you both."

"Off the record, so are we," O'Mara confirmed.

Pringle and her crew moved away, and Jo and O'Mara surveyed the scene before them. "How in the world are we going to get out of here?"

"We can do it. We won the Super Bowl together, didn't we?"

"We won more than that, lots and lots more."

"I know that, my love." He wrapped his arm more tightly around her.

"Now," she said, "see that opening there between the photographer in the blue jacket and that coach. If we sneak through there . . ."

"And around the camera crew—" he continued the strategy session "we'll make it."

"We certainly will."

They kissed once more and moved off together into the crush, knowing that it was first down and goal for them. Their quiet place and their brand-new life were only a few easily crossed inches away.

Harlequin Temptation

COMING NEXT MONTH

#145 LAUGHTER IN THE RAIN
Shirley Larson

Blake Lindstrom was a changed man—he'd been through hell. It took a small-town teacher like Jamie to show him what heaven on earth was all about....

#146 THE FAMILY WAY Jayne Ann Krentz

Though pregnant and unwed, fiesty Pru Kenyon wasn't about to marry the father of her child for appearance' sake. She wanted a love match with Case, or nothing at all....

#147 BIRDS OF A FEATHER Leigh Roberts

Adrien Spencer had great limbs!—and the rest of his redwood tree costume wasn't bad, either. But it was what was under all that bark that really intrigued Sarabeth....

#148 A WINNING COMBINATION
Maris Soule

When Alexis came home to Alaska, she had every intention of settling down. But then she met up with J. J. Callaway—sexy, adventurous and very *unsettling*....

PATRICIA MATTHEWS

America's First Lady of Romance upholds her long standing reputation as a bestselling romance novelist with . . .

Caught in the steamy heat of America's New South, Rebecca Trenton finds herself torn between two brothers—she yearns for one but a dark secret binds her to the other.

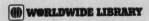

ATTRACTIVE, SPACE SAVING BOOK RACK

Display your most prized novels on this handsome and sturdy book rack. The hand-rubbed walnut finish will blend into your library decor with quiet elegance, providing a practical organizer for your favorite hard-or soft-covered books.

Only $9.95

Approximately 16" x 8" when assembled

Assembles in seconds!

To order, rush your name, address and zip code, along with a check or money order for $10.70* ($9.95 plus 75¢ postage and handling) payable to *Harlequin Reader Service*:

Harlequin Reader Service
Book Rack Offer
901 Fuhrmann Blvd.
P.O. Box 1325
Buffalo, NY 14269-1325

Offer not available in Canada.

BKR-1R

* New York residents add appropriate sales tax.